7/97

People on the Prowl

People
on the
Prowl

Short Stories
by

Jaime Collyer

translated by
Lillian Lorca de Tagle

Latin American Literary Review Press
Series: Discoveries
1996

The Latin American Literary Review Press publishes Latin American creative writing under the series title *Discoveries*, and critical works under the series *Explorations*.

Library of Congress Cataloguing-in-Publication Data

Collyer, Jaime.
    [Gente al acecho. English]
    People on the prowl: short stories / by Jaime Collyer; translated by Lillian Lorca de Tagle.
    p. cm. -- (Discoveries)
    ISBN 0-935480-73-0
    I. Tagle, Lillian. II. Title. III. Series.
PQ6653.0396G4613   1995
863--dc20   95-21099
                             CIP

Cover art by Lisette Miller. Author photograph by Bartolo Ortiz.

The paper used in this publication meets the minimum requirements of the American National Standard for Permanence of Paper for Printed Library Materials Z39.48-1984. ⊚

Latin American Literary Review Press
121 Edgewood Avenue • Pittsburgh, PA • 15218
Tel (412)371-9023 • Fax (412)371-9025

Acknowledgments

This project is supported in part by grants from the National Endowment for the Arts in Washington D.C., a federal agency, and the Commonwealth of Pennsylvania Council on the Arts.

*To Patricia, who crossed
the desert with me.*

contents

Loneliness is Satan's playing field

Vladimir Nabokov
Pale Fire

The episode that triggered everything was trivial. It may even be summarized in a few lines: after placing a prosthesis in his last patient's mouth, the prestigious orthodontist Hugo Schatzman—who also happens to be our neighbor in house #8 —leaves his office one afternoon to consult with his doctor about some "inexplicable fatigue" that overcomes him when awakening; the physician detects something more than a simple vitamin deficiency, orders X rays of the thorax, discovers a shadow in his left lung; a second physician orders more tests that will determine, after a week's time, whether Hugo is going to die of cancer or if he is only a banquet that the Koch bacillus has organized in his body. The bacillus can be kicked out, but cancer is a different matter altogether.

"Anyhow, I will have to quit smoking forever," the patient tells his friends and neighbors gathered in his home that evening. And he smiles, probably at the irony contained in the word "forever."

That first smile gives his future gestures a certain aura of greatness, a transcendent quality that will grow during the week, in the time we have left to confirm one or the other diagnosis: death or absolution.

Hugo is dying on us. This is the feeling, the sudden certainty that takes hold of us all.

"At present we have a shortage of martyrs," I comment that night to Sonia. "At least this is moving."

"Please," she reproaches me. "Haven't you thought about Ana Luisa and their child?"

"Of course," I acknowledge, feeling embarrassed. "Ana Luisa and the child, of course."

The next morning at breakfast I watch through the curtains as Hugo, who is up early, walks with determination toward his

Toyota. Ana Luisa follows him seconds later and wraps a scarf around his neck. Everyone else is also looking through their sheer curtains, worried about both of them, who look like a well-adjusted couple. His leaving early to work at his office is probably well thought out: it is necessary to start leaving early, take advantage of every light hour, wake up at dawn because the dark of night stalks Hugo,waiting to fall upon his neck and snatch him away from us. His unexpected doom gives him stature, while the rest of us hiding behind the curtains become prosaic and irrelevant.

That day he returns later than usual and we all go out to greet him, with Ana Luisa. There is a morbid quality in the way we all pat him on the shoulder and make contrived jokes about the doctor's diagnosis. Somebody compares him to Marguerite Gautier and promises to give him a bouquet of camellias next Monday, a suggestion we all laughingly approve. The emphasis is obviously on tuberculosis, a collective strategy designed to dispel the other option, the frightening possibility of seeing Hugo in the hospital in a few months, penetrated by tubes, and then carrying him later in a horizontal position to the cemetery.

Grateful for the jokes that act as a soothing balm to the pain that awaits her, Ana Luisa invites us for a drink, a suggestion that Hugo is delighted to agree to. At house #8 we are all overcome by a feeling of paradoxical conformity. We realize at that hour of dusk, as the dying man's serenity dazzles us, that nothing, not even our friend's death, will take our futures away from us. The young women look at him surreptitiously. Some allow themselves to make brief eye contact with him. Death, the possibility of death, enhances his attractiveness. In their mind's eye his body becomes a perishable material that must be captured visually (with their hands, too?) because soon it will be no more. We shall know on Monday. In the meantime, let's drink a toast.

Nobody wants to leave. Near midnight, under the influence of rum and vermouth, I happen to comment on the news of the trial of Winnie Mandela in Cape Town.

"And why is she on trial?" Hugo inquires. "What is she accused of?"

"Beating a couple of blacks to death in an alley," I explain. "She alone beat to death a couple of blacks? I thought that's what DeKlerk's government was for. Or any other bastard in his place."

"Her bodyguards, Winnie's bodyguards also contribute to the quota."

A heavy silence follows.

"In that case, apartheid is preferable, don't you think?" I suggest. "The government passes sentence in court, but the condemned may appeal. With the bodyguard, a six-foot black with a club in his hands, there is no possible recourse. Later he goes to Winnie and tells the story in his own way: 'I just had to kill him, Chief.'"

My explanation provokes a certain malaise among those present, shakes the crumbling wall of our convictions, now that our army of old rebels has been gradually decimated by government and public institutions. Sonia watches me from a corner of the room with a grimace of displeasure on her face. She is an unconditional fan of Winnie Mandela, that much is obvious. Those two black guys must have done something wrong to deserve being taken into the alley.

"I don't believe it," says Hugo finally.

"Neither do I," the others echo in a chorus.

Death, even as conjecture, favors unanimity. Somebody alludes to "the manipulation of news by international agencies," a hypothesis that pleases everybody and Winnie is absolved without even having to appear in court. I am careful to keep my mouth shut for the remainder of the gathering, which lasts almost until 2 o'clock. Nobody is paying attention to the time. Such a meeting may never occur again.

Returning home along the gravel path, Sonia expresses her disapproval.

"Why did you bring up the Winnie Mandela trial tonight? Did you think it appropriate, under the circumstances?"

"What circumstances?"

For a minute, she is baffled. What circumstances?

"I don't know," she concludes. "It didn't seem proper to bring up the story of the two black men dropped in an alley."

"Well, all right. It might be better not to delve into such subjects around Hugo."

This time I yield easily, with the sole purpose of insuring myself a peaceful night's sleep. Once in bed, I fail to fall asleep, just as may be happening to the others in their respective houses. At dawn, the night already wasted, I reach some convictions: I regret being healthy, which is also probably the case with the others; I regret not having a decaying lung to spark some measure of consensus among friends and make me enigmatic and attractive to my female neighbors.

On Thursday, four days before the final diagnosis, we repeat the get-together in our home. Hugo increases the attention paid to him with unexpected maneuvers. He tells us that he left his office early—premolars and cavities don't interest him anymore—and spent several hours at the National Library researching the deaths of famous men. Among others, he mentions Nelson, wounded by enemy fire at Trafalgar, torn to pieces in the arms of his faithful orderly, before whom he utters only one sentence: "The kiss of death, Horatio." He mentions Sergei Essenin, facing a mirror in his hotel room, his veins cut, writing his last poem with his own blood: "Good-bye my friend, in this life dying is nothing new...." Finally, he mentions Mahatma Gandhi, who forgives his assassin before dying. These descriptions bring tears to Ana Luisa's eyes. The rest of us keep silent. This time, everyone retires early, in a reflective mood.

At night, when she thinks I am asleep, I hear Sonia crying in the dark. Once again, I regret the lack of a bacillus in my body. Any kind would do.

The next evening, I run into Hugo returning home, just as he emerges from his Toyota. He sees me and offers a melancholy smile, with that contrived air of languor that has clung to his face in the last few days. I find him distant, a sure sign that new changes have occurred within him. This time it's something big: it happened in his office, a kind of "satori," a primordial revelation, precisely when he was about to fill a patient's tooth with gutta-percha, in this instance, someone named Gutiérrez.

"It never happened to me before," he says, still surprised.

"Have you read Borges? *The Aleph?*"

"Of course."

"It was something like that. A sudden realization of everything that is and everything that has existed."

Aware of his enthusiasm, I let him unburden himself about his own Aleph as he discovered it in Gutiérrez's mouth, on one side of the epiglottis.

"That's complicated," I say. "How will you be able to continue your observations?"

"I shall prolong his treatment," he says without remorse. "I will find as many cavities as necessary. But let me tell you what I saw..."

His terminology disappoints me. As was to be expected, he expounds on the "incessant and vast universe" and speaks about "a center to which all centers converge." Too well known, even to myself, who never reads any writer twice, not even Borges.

On Saturday we all get together again at our house. Hugo takes advantage of the opportunity to reveal to the others his discovery in Gutiérrez's mouth, leaving them dazzled. Death, for others a defeat, is in his case a silver thread, a jump into metaphysics, although the items he suggests in his patient's mouth seem quite unappealing to me. Borges talked about cobwebs in old religious sites, unreachable deserts, playing cards, tigers and retreating armies. Schatzman speaks about all the games played by second-rate teams last year, his mother's closets in Melipilla, about all the molars he has pulled out during his many years of practice. He doesn't evoke infinity but his audience listens respectfully to his enumeration.

"And Gutiérrez's gutta-percha?" I finally ask. "With all that Aleph floating around in his mouth, you must have put it in his eye, for sure."

The audience turns to look at me with disapproval. Sonia offers more wine and canapés to ease the tension and gives me a homicidal look.

Sunday, nearing the final verdict, our spirits are depressed and we each seek refuge in our own home. Ignorant of the impending event, the children play noisily until sundown in the gravel-covered yard. Their voices, their usual fights, seem distant to us, unreal, as Hugo Schatzman's name will sound to us once we have lost him. It's cloudy and it's Sunday, two good reasons to stay at home now that the wait for the diagnosis enters the final countdown. Tomorrow we will know: death or resurrection, according to the laboratory's verdict.

In the end, everything turns out less dramatic than we expected. That evening, Ana Luisa and Hugo arrive, smiling, arms around each other. We all step out to welcome them.

"Tuberculosis!" Hugo announces and we take turns hugging him.

The lung can still be repaired with a number of punctures, the appropriate medicines and some rest.

The next evening, we celebrate the good news at his house. Somebody purchases a bouquet of camellias that is given to Hugo on behalf of all of us. Jokes surface with the champagne and other niceties, but nobody finds them that amusing, now that we only have a demoted stereotype of Marguerite Gautier to laugh about without enthusiasm. Hugo tries sincerely to renew the mystique, to regain an air of tragedy. He points out that laboratories sometimes make mistakes. He insists on the Aleph issue, but someone asks him, pointedly this time, about the gutta-percha in poor Gutiérrez's mouth. Laughter drowns him out before he can even start to enumerate what he has found, so far, in his patient's throat.

That night, once again, I can't sleep. Neither can Sonia. I hear her turn and sigh impatiently in the dark.

"Don't you think that he looks very thin?" she finally asks.

"Who?"

"Hugo. He really looks as though he were terminal."

In that instant, I understand what will happen. In the next days, nobody talks about Hugo, who is referred to just by his last name: Schatzman, the one in house #8. The moron who was going to die. His recurring presence every afternoon offends us, as well as the yet imperceptible detail that he might be gaining weight and recuperating. We feel shocked by his confident attitude, which now seems trivial to us, making us trivial, too. We wanted him terminal and transcendent, not immortal.

Someone talks—facetiously—about running him down

with a car if the Koch bacillus fails. It is rumored that the suggestion originated with Ana Luisa herself. Better a traffic martyr than a dentist with a bad lung, say I, says she.

It's not a bad idea, say I.

pharaoh exposed

"You shall live again!" a high priest of Thebes whispered at the last moment during the Pharaoh's funeral. "Forever and ever, young again!" A deliberate litany against death, the funerary slogan reproduced optimistically on the walls of the royal crypt and every subterranean mausoleum along the Nile, to encourage the corpse of the day to proceed on his long voyage to the depths of the night, and assist him in reappearing on the new day from within his own mummified remains. I know, with some sudden horror, that at least one— one of those illustrious cadavers of four thousand years ago— did return, did live again. Fed up with endless nights, weary of immortality, he told me the story himself in a Cairo bar.

Bancroft and I had already spent three years in Sheikh Abd el-Gurna, a village infested by scarabs where we were digging on behalf of the Royal London Society for Egyptian Explorations, under the rather foolish but tenacious eye of tourists. Food was scarce and pitiful, although the scarabs were of the opposite opinion. Water threatened us with treacherous diarrhea and London often forgot our fees, but the laborers and natives harassed us anyhow, every day when we left our adobe hut, expecting a tip (*Baksheesh, sahib, baksheesh!*)—just not to break the habit, since they had little trust in the amount still left in our pockets.

We used to ride on mules between our improvised home and the Valley of the Kings, that underground labyrinth of tombs and sepulchers scattered over the area. Bancroft, an octogenarian already sated with Egypt, complained about the fares or the bucking of the mule, the scorching sun or the tourists. As we penetrated deeper into the Valley of the Kings, he usually gave up on the mule and jumped grumbling off its back, a gesture that didn't save him from paying the muleteer the agreed fare to our destination. After the customary haggling, sweating profusely and stumbling on the way, he would go to the only refreshment stand in the area. He would sit down at a table and ask Ibrahim, the owner, for a beer. I would watch this maneuver in silence. Then I, resignedly, would ride off on my mule. Whenever I looked back, the deserter raised his glass in my honor, urging me on to proceed alone to the excavations, in both our names. I would think of his mother in the least flattering terms.

Fortunately, I didn't complain about his frequent desertions. One day in November, a miracle occurred and the beer stand caved in, dragging its four tables, Bancroft included, into the hole. Ibrahim sustained minor lesions and second degree trauma due to several Pepsi-Cola cases that crashed on his shaved cranium. Bancroft came out unharmed, after sliding into the void of a sepulcher hidden precisely beneath the beer stand. This was the entrance to a quadrangular chamber that had been waiting there for thirty centuries, apparently untouched. Waiting for Bancroft and me.

Before the place swarmed with tourists, my colleague took possession of the site, clamoring for a physician to take care of Ibrahim's head.

"Poor man," he commented, "he will obviously have to change his trade."

"At least move somewhere else."

"We'll have to take all this to Cairo. We must hire a barge."

"All this" was the sarcophagus we found in the burial chamber after extricating Ibrahim from the hole and opening the access to the crypt with shovels. The sarcophagus was covered with hieroglyphs, inscriptions, fragments of the Amduat, the Book of the Night, and images of the goddess Nut, the deity who every morning resurrected the day and brought the pharaoh out of the night. It was surrounded by bronze statuettes sculpted millennia ago, wooden amulets, small mummified animals, clothes and jewelry worn by the dignitary buried there, and emblems of his power.

The stone sarcophagus was sealed. A week later, in the presence of local authorities and media correspondents from all over the world, we opened it with great solemnity. Inside was hidden a second sarcophagus of solid gold within which, according to the wall inscriptions, lay the mummified body of Nat-Hotep, King of the Twenty-first Dynasty. The sight of the dazzling metallic inner coffin prompted an admiring murmur among the spectators. Bancroft and I solemnly lifted the metal lid. The collective murmur turned into a shocked exclamation; much to Bancroft's and my own perplexity and that of our guests, Nat-Hotep's inner sarcophagus was empty.

"He's gone!" commented the BBC correspondent. "He's out on a stroll!"

Bancroft immediately felt that he was the target of dark suspicions. The press conference took place then and there, at the pit's entrance, with my colleague and me cornered by a tide of camera flashes and reporters avidly awaiting an explanation. A few minutes after the first questions, the *National Geographic* writer suggested, with obvious malice in his tone of voice, in reference to the empty sarcophagus:

"We know today that Lord Carnavon and his assistant opened the sepulcher of Tutankhamen, on their own authority and at their own risk, before showing it to the press and presenting us with their discovery. I ask myself if the elusive Nat-Hotep, who is now missing, has not suffered similar profanation and whether somebody has taken his mummified body out for a promenade. Along with some pieces of gold, of course!"

As could be expected, Bancroft burst into a rage, threatened the man from the *National Geographic* with his fist and suggested the possibility of answering his malicious suggestions in court, for the time being demanding an apology. At that point an autumn downpour was unleashed, and we had to postpone the conference to wall up the tomb's entrance to protect it from flooding. The Egyptian Tourism Police would stand guard over the treasures until the time came to transport them to Cairo, specifically to the Antiquities Museum.

That evening, at coffee time, I talked over the incident with Bancroft.

"It's not fair," I said.

"What?"

"What that guy suggested this afternoon."

"At the press conference? He's a bastard."

"Anyhow, it's strange," I added. "The sarcophagus being empty."

"Perhaps the body was taken a long time ago," he pointed out, discouraged, "several centuries ago and then they sealed everything up again."

"Who?"

"Who knows. His subjects, Nat-Hotep's people. The vandals of that time. The ransacking of tombs is nothing new, Williamson. Any of those who participated in building the sepulcher thousands of years ago could have returned after a few weeks to take anything they craved, and why not the Pharaoh too? Perhaps they threw him into a common grave that we may yet discover."

That might be true. Anyhow, the rumor of the Pharaoh's disappearance from his grave spread among the natives in the simple impulse to increase the arsenal of local superstitions, which held a directly proportionate relation to the affluence of tourists.

Two weeks after the failed press conference we finished the inventory and diagrams of the tomb, and carefully took down the stone sarcophagus, with the other coffin inside, before taking it to the wharf. The river journey, escorted by the Tourism Police patrol boat, was briefer than expected. We were sailing with the current toward Cairo. On the banks of the Nile, among rushes and palm trees, the peasants lined up to see us glide by and a flock of lateen-sailed feluccas came every so often to meet us, escorting us northward downriver. The women sang ancestral tunes and men shot their hunting rifles into the air as a last homage to the king whose sarcophagus we carried— the last pharaoh, who now prompted the multitudinous honors from his new rural subjects on both river banks, most of whom were unaware of his absence on board.

From the beginning of our voyage, Bancroft was affected by the river's swinging motion, multiplying his digestive outbursts on deck and into the greenish surface of the Nile. In Cairo, in the safety of the wharves, he completely gave up. Surrounded by a swarm of porters and port laborers, he revealed his decision:

"It's all over, Williamson. I'm going back to London, to

lecture on whatever might cross my mind. I am fed up with Egypt and its relics. You can take over getting all this to the museum and writing the catalog. Not forgetting to include my name, of course."

We solemnly shook hands to conclude at last our several years of research, which the museum catalog would ratify in some shabbily edited paragraphs. Bancroft left the wharf, dragging his feet, an old pachyderm, too weak to lead the herd, only followed now by a trail of dockworkers and beggars intent on getting a coin from him. For some reason they preferred him, like flies drawn to dung.

Negotiations at the museum in Cairo took considerably longer than the river voyage from Thebes. Just to get the museum authorities to take care of the transfer from the docks to the institution took a whole week and a hard bargaining session with officials and porters, half in Arabic and half in English. The statuettes and other decorative artifacts were scattered at random in a room at the end of the northwest hall. As to the Nat-Hotep sarcophagus, the interim director of the museum decided that it already had enough of the kind and he ordered it confined to the basement of the building, together with dozens of mummified small animals and tablets with hieroglyphics still to be deciphered. Despite my disappointment, on the seventh day I rested.

***

It happened two weeks later, for no reason whatsoever, one Sunday at nightfall. At that hour I left the hotel heading for the famous Liberation Square and from there, following the riverbank, to the Dakar, a nightclub where mirrors multiply the lustful performance of the belly dancers or the juggling of a Lebanese acrobat on the tightrope. The mostly Egyptian audience sat in pairs or threesomes, more or less circumspect or noisy, depending on how thoroughly they observed the Koranic ban on alcohol, elbows on the small tables inlaid with mother-of-pearl, slowly sipping a beer or a mint infusion until the wee hours of dawn. Entertainment that night included a Tunisian magician who filled the stage with doves and bunches of flowers, ending his performance by throwing fire out of his mouth. The final act would be Layla Abudi, "Queen of the Night" as the announcer qualified her, with little originality, through his megaphone. Moments later the girl bore out the cliché, contorting her way between the tables, arching backwards to nearly touch with her lips the glass of some lonely customer in the shadows of the bar.

It was Layla and her bumpy passage between the tables that made me fix my attention on him: a solitary individual in a corner, resembling a character sprung from a silent movie, his hair smoothed and parted in the middle, shining with brilliantine in the spotlights, in a white suit, fine silk shirt and slender black velvet bow tie. He remained imperturbable at his table, drinking with extreme deliberation from a glass of anisette, totally indifferent to Layla's provocations and belly shaking, acknowledging her only with a toast by the slightest waving of his hand, hardly lifting his glass.

The place cleared out little by little by early morning, reduced to the hour's usual deadweights: a wilted American with glazed eyes, nodding at the bar, and several Egyptian customers who, drowsy from hashish, muttered illegal transactions while on the stage a local singer performed after a fortuitously short announcement on the loudspeaker. Close to 2 A.M., the proprietor brought an intriguing message, scrawled on a napkin by the customer at the back table wearing the white suit and a stony smile. I detected in his handwriting a smattering of obsolescence, like autumn leaves kept between the pages of a book that we discover again after many years. In a couple of English sentences, he referred to the honor it would be for him to share his table with a prestigious archeologist such as I, if I were to accept his offer for a drink.

"Do you know him?" I asked the proprietor.

"It's a Mr. Hamed," he explained, "an old customer of ours."

"Should I accept?"

"Never refuse such an invitation from an Egyptian."

As I approached his table, I appraised the sallow hue of his complexion, the shadows under his eyes, a certain bilious coloring of his face, in addition to the deadly seriousness of his features. He stood up and extended his hand, cold and bony as was to be expected. He ordered a brandy for me and another anisette for himself. He hesitated for a moment in deep silence and then spoke in a lugubrious voice.

"I'll get straight to the point, Williamson. Let us not talk for the time being about the discovery you just made in Thebes. I am interested mainly in the influential position you now enjoy in Cairo. For a man who belongs to another time, like me, trying to acquire some influence could be very chancy. You understand me?"

"No."

"I think you do," he stated, smiling for the first time. "You are a member of the Society for Egyptian Explorations, isn't that so? Like your friend, that nonagenarian...what is his name?"

"Bancroft," I answered with irritation. "As to his age, he isn't that old. No fault of his."

"No, of course," he acceded. "Wouldn't I know!"

This last sentence seemed gratuitous to me. In spite of his run down physique, he couldn't be more than 48, 50 at the most.

"Well?" I said.

"I shall get straight to the point," he said once more.

"I wish you would."

"My name now is Hamed," he went on, "before that I was Rasul and a long time ago, Nakht. I have been a beggar in the outskirts of Cairo, chief assistant to the Mameluke sultan and whatever you may think of. You already know what my name and rank were before."

I was confused.

"You shall live again!" he exclaimed, "young again forever and ever! It worked, Williamson!"

"I don't understand..."

"Use your imagination, my friend. Go back a couple of weeks to Thebes. It's not much to ask considering how long it took you and Bancroft to explore the Valley of the Kings. Until the old man sat down one morning to drink some beer, as he did every day, and the ground caved in under him. It's enough to die laughing, Williamson, to think about that glorious coincidence:

the collapse of the beverage stand, just there, and the discovery of the sarcophagus! I waited three thousand years for it to happen."

"Listen to me, I..." I said, ready to reprimand him for drinking too much anisette and then leave his table as quickly as possible.

"I am the item missing at the museum, Williamson," he interrupted me.

"You..."

"My name, the real one, is Nat-Hotep."

***

Some time later, in the very early hours of the day, both of us dulled from brandy and anisette, I stopped caring about the credibility or lack of precision of his story, because I had become unsteady, in the darkness of the Dakar, and was unable to judge with certainty the accuracy of the speaker's dates, which he expounded on with total assertiveness, without faltering. He talked about the empire and the invasions that he and his generals had to drive back on the river's delta, a natural bastion against the barbarians rushing in from the Mediterranean. He talked about his own demise as a result of liver failure, a crisis that none of his priests was able to avert, and later his unexpected resurrection. Unexpected even by him.

"I woke up on the fourth day," he explained in a muffled voice, "wrapped in bandages, in the grave that you and Bancroft discovered. It had worked, Williamson."

"What are you talking about?"

"The return trip, with the goddess Nut leading me by the hand, and all that. You know this better than I do."

"And then what did you do?"

"I left the crypt, naturally. I was careful to seal it properly and departed to Thebes where I expected to have some fun. I was tired of being a Pharaoh. Once in the Valley of the Kings, I adopted the personality of Nakht, a humble peasant."

His wandering and arbitrary memory recalled the later—much later—arrival of the Arabs in Alexandria ("People who, unfortunately, only knew about camels"), the crumbling of the lighthouse, the destruction of the library. He had been at the

Nile's delta when the Crusaders landed ("To suggest that we worship a raving maniac nailed to a cross, can you imagine?") and by way of flattery, he became the Secretary to the Mameluke sultan, authorizing on his behalf a number of executions that he didn't seem to regret.

"During thirty or more centuries of life," he explained, ordering another anisette, "a hundred heads on one's account is of little concern."

He spoke kindly about Napoleon, whose harangue near the pyramids he had occasion to witness. As a son of the sun, he could easily understand imperial whims.

"He was a comedian," he summarized at four in the morning. "Power is but entertainment, a musical comedy financed by the people and Bonaparte knew his role well, even in defeat. By that time, I was called Rasul, Abdel Rasul, and I worked as a spy on behalf of the French against the Egyptian authorities. What a great experience."

"In what way?"

"The taste of treason, Williamson, you British know about it. Just think of what you did to Faisal."

"That was Lawrence's fault," I jumped, in a spontaneous fit of patriotism. "Lawrence promised him too much."

"If you say so...Anyhow, I was later forgiven. Immortality has advantages," he said, without elation, almost depressed. And he added, sighing, "But I'm tired. By the turn of the century, I decided to call myself Hamed and try my luck by joining the Independence Movement. To no avail, everything hopelessly bores me. That is why tonight I requested your company for this unsolicited history lesson."

"I don't understand."

"When I left the grave, I took pains to leave everything as it was, sealed from the outside, so nobody would notice my absence."

"So...?"

"I forgot where the tomb was, Williamson! I returned to Thebes a century and a half later, but the sand had covered any clues as to the location of the grave and the empire had gone to the dogs. The Persians were at the border. Loathsome people, believe me. I had nothing to do but hang around, Williamson, during thirty long centuries, until I read in the paper about your friend's accident when the ground caved in at the beer joint, and the transfer of the findings to Cairo. Now do you understand?"

"More or less."

"You are an archeologist of prestige," he said. "You could settle things for me, do the required setup and find the poison."

"What for?" I asked, alarmed.

He looked at me for a moment with a weary expression.

"So I can return to my sarcophagus," he said.

At that instant, the proprietor of the Dakar announced that it was time to close the bar.

"I want to die, Williamson." My companion spoke with precision. "I want to die again."

***

The London media considered it an exceptional event: the sudden discovery of the cadaver of a man dead three thousand years ago or more from a liver ailment (although there were additional indications of poisoning), in an archeological grave on the outskirts of Cairo where my unfailing Egyptologist's instincts had led me—according to the *Times*—in a relentless search for the famous Nat-Hotep, the pharaoh whose remains had been stolen, for indecipherable reasons, from his tomb in Thebes. It was almost impossible to explain to anyone how he had been preserved, considering the lack of bandages and other signs of mummification, but the *Times* didn't really care and the Sunday readers cared even less. In the long run, somebody attributed it to the relative lack of oxygen inside the grave. The Cairo Museum's catalog, which I wrote myself, refers without ambiguity to Nat-Hotep, whose sarcophagus was finally elevated to the main floor and main hall, Pharaoh included. The catalog mentions my name side by side with that of the King, giving me credit for the stupendous investigation that led to the discovery and identification of the body. At the last minute, I forgot to include Bancroft's name. But this is of little concern since, at present, he doesn't even recognize his own housekeeper.

I remember the first time I saw you, on the day scheduled for visitors, from four to six, in accordance with the prison's unappealable rules. It was in the yard that ironically displays its greenery by the jail's barred door, around which the women usually gather to visit their less upright sons, those addicted to the knife and other people's belongings, all of them waiting for the regulation frisking, the guards shouting at the crowd and the visitors cackling their indignation; the usual routine. I remember you that day, so young, so shy, standing back in a corner of the yard, keeping your distance from the other women, holding a bag of groceries, nervously stroking it while you thought— this is a hypothesis—that it would soon be four o'clock and wondering how this, your first experience with the unyielding arm of the law, would turn out (somebody talked about the frisking at the hands of the guards, indispensable requirement before entering the visiting room), finally meeting again with Salazar, your fiancé at the time, separated by the hateful table placed between the prisoners and the civilized world every Thursday. I detected something special, indescribable, in the way you distanced yourself from the group, the sidelong glances at the guard towers and barred windows, in one of which I stood, waiting for just about anything except a visitor.

Nobody in my family seemed even mildly interested in my case since I landed in this place, after going through all the usual formalities: frontal and profile pictures and a number that replaced forever, more or less, my name and my freedom. I'm not complaining. If one day I decided to take part in the domestic printing of money, the "done deal" that Fabrizio promised would bring us paradise, that decision was mine alone. I will not try again to justify my actions, as I did desperately before the judge, nor would I blame my relatives.

My home atmosphere was the best, and if the kid ends up hopelessly flawed, that's another story. With your unique presence at the prison on visitors' day, I came to realize that it was not necessary to have my pockets always full of money—least of all with bills printed at Fabrizio's place—at the risk of spending almost ten years here, behind bars.

I see you again now, redolent of that adolescent air that at the time seemed already about to turn: a child forced to grow up without fair warning, because Salazar, the fiancé, had startled everyone when he acted on the odd idea of threatening an upright citizen with a gun in an urban alley, when coincidentally, the police sprung a surprise on Salazar by catching him in the act. I could see in your face that you wanted to run away from the jail and never again follow the lead of a guy who failed one day to show up for a date when you thought that everything was right between you two. Then somebody brought a newspaper to the house and there it was in all its crude details: Salazar, your impetuous Romeo in the crime pages. Deep shadows under his eyes, looking haggard in the photo, and I told you, child, that scoundrel was no good for you. A mother is never wrong.

A week later you were in front of the prison (what would mother say?) waiting to save the scoundrel from the shadows at 4 o'clock, that unforgettable Thursday when you decided to join the group of visitors. I'm in a tower cell, one with a view of the yard from where I watched with delight your emergence from the avenue leading to the prison, your face so pale and sad, perfectly distinct among the crowd and the other visitors.

Those who had no visitors were allowed to remain in the rooms adjoining the barracks where the prisoners met their relatives. I stayed there every Thursday, standing by one of the access doors, a short distance from the place where you and Salazar met to speak. From there, chain smoking, I watched you out of the corner of my eye, looking at your delicate hands that Salazar nostalgically caressed. Once in a while you would look to the place where I was leaning against the wall, I remember it well, but I averted my eyes to some place in the courtyard, because of modesty, you know.

Life in prison goes on at a slow, parsimonious pace. Soon

I started to live for visitors' day, just like Salazar, clinging to the idea that you did know about me, the guy jailed forever—or almost—in the tower cell. At the time, when I consented to join the low-lifes—the fault of Fabrizio and his brilliant proposals—I had a premonition that things would go wrong, I sensed the bars, the loneliness of a tower cell, this life restricted to four unhealthy walls, all of it in order to wander through the city for a while with the deceptive smile of a millionaire.

It couldn't go on forever. Nothing lasts forever, they say, and it's true. It happened to Salazar one day. He came running into the courtyard where we were stretching our legs, his face distorted with joy.

"I'm leaving!" he yelled. "They gave me a pardon!"

"Leaving when?" I asked with fake enthusiasm.

"On Wednesday."

It would be the day before visiting day. I spent the whole week searching for an alternative, but there was none. I even considered the possibility of confiding in Salazar and begging him to stay at least until Thursday. But it was useless, there is no request strong enough to keep a man behind bars once his sentence is over, and early on Wednesday morning Salazar left the prison, taking away with him the joyous possibility of seeing you one last time, just once more.

The next day, Thursday, I found myself again absently leaning against the bars at the window, watching the courtyard. The women had already been there for an hour. At the stroke of four, they picked up their belongings and walked toward the prison entrance where they would be frisked. I was desolate as I looked down the avenue that led to the prison, the rows of trees, a group of children playing some unidentifiable game in the distance. And then I stretched out on my bunk and counted my last cigarettes.

A few seconds later, I heard the martial clicking of a guard's heels in the corridor, and saw him stop at the threshold of my cell.

"To the barracks, Jorquera," he ordered. "You have a visitor."

I don't know how I got downstairs except that I made it in record time, and sitting at the far corner of the table, I cried a little, like a baby, in your hands.

As for Salazar, your mother already had told you, that man was no good for you. And a mother is never wrong.

His real name was Godoy. I contributed to his changing it, for reasons of basic survival. According to the information I got from third parties, he came from some impoverished village at the side of an abandoned highway. In the capital, he graduated as a veterinarian in fewer years than normally required. At the university he gave proof of his impassioned nature, which time eventually changed. During a faculty strike he personally led a group of students determined to intimidate someone who refused to support the strike. Together they carried him to the head of the stairs and threatened to throw him down, preferably head first. Somebody, probably Godoy, decided at the last minute that this was rather extreme and the hostage was allowed to return to his classes unharmed.

When a counteroffensive and reprisals took place, Godoy chose to hide and leave the country, urged by his cohorts, who languished—we did languish—in clandestinity under the military boot. I was in charge of the liaison with "documentation and appearances," and responsible for suggesting a name change. Those at documentation agreed. He had to follow the usual procedure, they said. At the end of October I looked in the telephone directory for the right choice for an alternative, respectable last name. In the R's I found a Theodore Rosenblitt, dentist. Something told me that it would work well. The next day I went to the civil registrar's office, lied about a distant kinship with Rosenblitt and requested his birth certificate. He was eight years older than Godoy, who at the time must have been about thirty-five.

"No problem," our documentation person told me that night. "It's just a matter of frowning a bit when they take the photos, so he looks older. Besides, we make him wear a tie. The authorities are very particular about ties."

Godoy himself was not so sure when I explained this to him in the tiny room to which he was confined, feeling tired of hiding and clandestinity.

"Why didn't you look for a veterinarian like me?" he asked.

"What will I do if I have to pull teeth, wherever I go?"

"You offer to pull dogs' teeth," I answered. "Don't be so picky. Anyhow, here are the details about Rosenblitt's background that you will have to memorize."

A week later he finally flew to Mexico. When he left his hiding place we hugged him briefly and someone from the liaison team took him to the airport, where he passed the customs gate and the International Police inspection, without a hitch, wearing a maroon tie.

Ten long years elapsed before my turn came to seek refuge in the hiding place, after having distributed a large number of innocuous leaflets at the entrance of an official institution. An error of judgment: some ambitious employee in search of a quick promotion delivered a verbal description of my appearance to the counterinsurgency services. I decided to hide, while those in documentation searched for a suitable candidate to place on my passport. I got a lawyer from a wealthy district, author of publications in professional journals, with a Ph.D. from Balliol College in Oxford, a highly cultivated individual. Someone from the liaison group started a surveillance shift on his house in the suburbs to make sure that he was a conventional citizen. He was indeed, except for one characteristic: he limped slightly on his left leg. His birth certificate also indicated that he was one or two years older than I.

"You just frown a bit for the photos and that's it," the guy in charge of documentation, a congenital optimist, said to me.

In the loneliness of my hiding place, in front of a mirror, I tried to look older, like a man with works published in professional journals, an Oxford Ph.D. with a slight limp in the left leg. I even thought it was humorous. This was probably due to the comedian we all carry within us, waiting for our call to step on the stage. The hiding place was little more than a closet, with an electric burner and a bathroom on one side, all of it in small scale. Someone had left behind some old magazines dating back several years, a complete set of Gramsci's works, enough rice to feed an army for ten years and a cheap record player. There was only one small record, by Aretha Franklin: "I Say a Little Prayer." On the fifth day of listening to it, twice in the morning and twice again in the evening, it started to sound like a requiem. I thought I had a better understanding of Godoy's frustration which, ten years earlier, had seemed superfluous to me, an affectation on his part.

Shortly afterward, the liaison group managed to get me a visa for Mexico, a country that accepted without squeamishness an attorney trained at Oxford. I flew there in early summer. I was looking forward with pleasure to Godoy's reception at the airport, but only a veteran of exile (whom I thought long dead) and a woman had been assigned to meet me. She said her name was Liliana and described the situation in few words: work was scarce, but they would take care of the requirements to get me the work permit by way of their contacts in high places, following payment of the amount agreed upon for such cases. It would be best for me to hold on to my false identity until the time it would be opportune to return to the "interior," when it would help me get past the police controls on arrival.

When we were leaving the airport highway, I asked if they could recommend a reasonably priced boarding house.

"We have taken care of that," said Liliana, proud of her own efficiency. "You will stay for a while with Rosenblitt. Do you know him?"

"Rosenblitt?" I asked, surprised. "I think so. I was in charge of establishing contacts with documentation when he was in hiding."

"So much the better. You will stay with him in his apartment until you find your own accommodations. Do you have a family? Children?"

"No. I mean, yes, but they are staying with their mother."

"Great. Fewer problems for everyone concerned."

Rosenblitt—not Godoy anymore—distant and reserved, greeted me at the threshold of his apartment, a large flat with big windows in a wealthy neighborhood of the federal capital. The place was a true reflection of his curiously meticulous character, which I quickly perceived as I watched him prepare coffee in the kitchen where the coffee pot and the sugar bowl were in their assigned spots, everything in their assigned place, every motion strictly as needed. He had put on weight and lost much of his hair. He looked like some leader in an official history or a martyr in uniform, like those whose profiles appear on coins and who storm the government's palaces before reaching the rank of colonel. He spoke little. As in the past, he seemed more comfortable with silence.

"What happened?" he inquired, stirring his coffee. "Did they catch you?"

"No. I distributed some pamphlets in front of the Department of Transportation. Two days later an arrest order was issued."

"Bad luck."

"A miscalculation."

Watching him parsimoniously sip his coffee, I tried to figure his age. He must be about 45 now, but the indelible marks of exile were evident in his eyes, tired and rheumy. A certain fatigue in his movements gave an impression of older age. A man eight years older.

"And what about you?" I inquired in turn, in a jesting mood. "Have you pulled many teeth?"

"Quite a few," he said without hesitation, and I laughed at this assertion. After all, the dentist was the real Rosenblitt.

A week later I found out it was not so—not just a simple witticism—when I returned unexpectedly one evening and surprised him sitting in his armchair, his eyeglasses on the tip of his nose, lost in contemplation of a plaster cast that looked like a maxilla.

"What's that?" I asked.

"A typical case," he explained. "One or two molars that don't fit the lower ones, which alters the bite. The lack of contact weakens the root. Before you are 60 years old half of the teeth drop out."

"How do you know all this?"

"It's the natural evolution of the dental plate," he said, laconic.

"Ah!"

His social life was limited. Nevertheless, two weeks after my arrival he invited to his apartment a couple he was acquainted with and several Mexican colleagues "from the clinic," sober people who talked about inflation and its devastating effects, who drank white wine in small doses with the oyster stew that he prepared himself; people who listened to Count Basie at a reasonable volume. The wine managed to loosen the tongue of our host, who took advantage of a pause at dessert and coffee time, to expound on the Talmud and the cyclopean works of Moses Mendelssohn, grandfather of the famous romantic composer, to whom, he explained, warming up to the subject, Frederick the Great himself forbade access to the Berlin Academy of Sciences.

By brandy time we separated into small groups to talk about different subjects. One of the guests, a specialist in maxilofacial surgery, whispered to me his conclusions under the protective complicity of Count Basie and his orchestra.

"This Theodore is a good chap." His tone anticipated some objection. "A pity that he is Jewish."

I wanted to dissent, but restrained myself. Theodore sat pensively at the opposite side of the room. His face was different from the one I knew a decade ago. He was an older man, serene, who would never throw academics down the stairs, and now just pulled teeth from nine to six. A man who had replaced Gramsci's complete works with the Talmud and the vast, elusive blame for the biblical deicide.

Some time later I rented my own apartment...when I had already begun to limp on my left foot.

all the horses in toulon go around naked*

Let it be perfectly clear that in these lines I don't pretend to judge the well-known Preceptor Maurice Sebastien Dufeu, nor those who sent him to the guillotine in the cruel, chaotic times of the Convention and the Jacobin terror. I am a historian, not a member of the holy league of pure souls. I only compile facts and records. I organize them on top of my desk, draw conclusions while not pretending to reach the absolute, but certainly aspiring to the undeniable sharpness of a photograph. I am more interested in the amount of megatons thrown over Hiroshima than the victims' wounds. I detest Maximilien de Robespierre far less than some of his countrymen do even today. He was above all a moralist, a slave to the same noble concepts that condemn him in history's memory. Because of them he sent Preceptor Dufeu to the scaffold. Because of them he followed him to the guillotine a short time later.

True to my academic habits, I must confess that my interest in the life and origins of Dufeu was arbitrary, by sheer chance initiated in a Paris fish shop; that no exhaustive study of the Revolution and its detailed incidents justifies the emphasis on his person; that if in the research of his obscure biography I exhausted the public funds long ago assigned to me (for a more ambitious project, of course) this was due to a strictly personal decision, based on a vague bewilderment that still lingers in my spirit. And only in my own spirit. In any case, my version of the Preceptor is supported by real facts and documents. Anyone who may want to investigate the affair will find in the municipal archives in Paris—in the brittle, yellowish folios that summarize the Revolution's terror in quick trials and abrupt sentences—a reference to "the case of citizen Dufeu," brief mentions of his birth in Toulon, his short stay in a monastery there,

*Jauja Short Story Award (Valladolid, Spain, 1985)

the prompt weakening of his monastic drift to adhere, once free of God, to the Paris bourgeoisie and the *sans-culottes* with whom he foresaw the Bastille's explosion. A well-known disciple of Rousseau, he knew how to spread his ideas with ferocity through pamphlets that circulated from hand to hand in the French capital, exposing the prevailing social disintegration or calling for the impending rebellion of "laborers" and "indigents" that would put an end to the frivolity and wastefulness of the gentry. His Genevan master was already an old man, fearful of his own ideas when Dufeu scurried through the streets demanding equality. With the money collected from his lessons to the offspring of noblemen—always faithful to his fifth columnist's fate—he financed the modest publication of the only text still preserved in the Parisian archives legitimized by his signature: "On the Moral and Sound Judgment in the Management of Human Societies," printed by the Tessier Brothers in 1791. His crystal clear and efficacious prose is far superior to the equivocal hesitations of his master. What in Rousseau appears as a desire for conciliation and equilibrium, in the Preceptor's pages stands out as a visceral nonconformity and a clear, definitive bet on the disintegration of the monarchic system. Such vehemence certainly had an influence on his anonymity and his ultimate sentencing by his former comrades in arms.

Many might reject the background preceding his encounter with the sharp reality of the guillotine. His whole life seems to concentrate on a last irreproachable gesture to the crowd gathered around the gallows on the day of his execution, the "8 Thermidor of year I" exactly, as it appears consigned in the Parisian archives according to the peculiar denominations of the Revolution's calendar. Nevertheless, I consider it essential to investigate the details of his marginal, passionate life. What is the point of delving into a man's final outcome without making minimal references to his previous troubles and failures. If Fleming discovered penicillin, it was probably after he saw a cousin die consumed by syphilis. If Dufeu shocked the crowd of spectators that summer day in 1793, today he deserves an exposition of his most intimate motivations. I know now what they were. I have read about them in his own handwriting in a damp fish shop on Rue Tolbiac, located a few meters from my office, where I write these lines. The name of the proprietor is Sebastien Dufeu. At first sight an anonymous district merchant, medium height, lively eyes and cordial expression—a rare attitude among Paris merchants—ruddy complexion and hands skilled in the skinning of hakes and bass. A specialist, a praiseworthy craftsman in a quiet trade he practices among the stench and viscera accumulated daily in the waste buckets of his shop. Now I know that he cares little about the assumed indignity of his profession, the fish odors that no detergent can obliterate from his hands. He is keenly aware that he belongs to a prolific race, being a contemporary heir of those who, like his great-grandfather's father, created with fire and blood the bourgeois system that now feeds his humble fishmonger's coffers. In fact, he is the most remote relative of Preceptor Maurice Sebastien Dufeu, who by the late eighteenth century generously spread the seed in the Parisian suburbs, among the laborers and the dispossessed he defended in his writings. An unsuspected chain of relationships and affairs culminated at Dufeu's fish shop. I met him by chance a few weeks ago. I had been in Paris since last spring. I would occasionally visit his establishment to buy a couple dozen oysters, maybe a lobster, a diversity of dying crustaceans one happens to find in a fish shop, still horribly waving their claws and dragging their shells in the shop's window. It was he who, to my unsuspected good fortune, led the conversation to my line of work.

"You are new in this neighborhood, eh?" he asked one morning in the lilting French of those raised in the south of the country, near the Pyrenees or the Mediterranean. "Do you work nearby?"

"I'm a historian. I do research at the municipal archives on a government assignment."

The reference to my specialty seemed to impress him, obviously distracting him from the mackerel he was torturing at that moment.

"History interests me," he said. "I'm not a specialist like you. I have to take care of this business, *non?*"

I felt a vague surge of affection toward that man, probably on account of the humility of his demeanor, the sincere awareness of his limitations. He probably had never stuck his nose in newspapers. He would have used the archives' publications to wrap his fish. But that didn't make me better than him. Of course he had to attend to his business.

"Which period are you studying?" he asked when I was about to leave his kingdom of scales and crustaceans.

"Modern times, the Revolution...the Napoleonic wars."

That's all we spoke about at the time. Two weeks later I stopped by his shop again: oysters are one of my most frequent gastronomic weaknesses.

"Aha! The historian," he exclaimed upon seeing me. "I'll be with you in a minute."

After finishing business with one of his customers, he advanced toward me.

"I have something that might interest you," he said, removing his apron and indicating with a slight nod of his head the way to the back of the shop. "Marcel! Stop whatever you are doing and take charge of the business!"

A red-haired lad with a sleepy expression on his face came from the cold storage room and stood obediently, although with little enthusiasm, behind the counter.

"I'm going to the back of the shop," said the proprietor. And then he addressed me, "Follow me. I want to show you something."

There was no point in refusing his invitation. The outright force of his gestures and his voice did not exclude a certain authoritarian quality, an inner pride, the secret satisfaction of a man who could afford to distract a few minutes from his professional routine to revert—with sober ostentation—to his double personality of merchant and descendant of some anonymous founder of the motherland's system. Although to me he was still the fishmonger from Rue Tolbiac.

"It's this way."

With a commanding gesture and an implacable smile he invited me to enter with him the corridor that led to a back door. It was dark and it smelled of fish, rotting wood and decaying spoils of something immemorial. Momentarily blinded in the darkness, I realized that all this was not a simple coincidence. That my legitimate weakness for oysters might well entail the mysterious possibility of a transmigration. It's not in just any Parisian fish shop that you find an anonymous messenger waiting for you, hidden in the depths of an interior passageway holding an unexpected fragment of a unique and authentic part of history. After groping our way for several meters, we finally reached a door.

"Here it is," he said advancing ahead of me and taking a bunch of keys out of his pocket. Used to the penumbra of the passageway, he opened the door without difficulty and invited me to step in. When he turned on the light and once I was able to overcome the first blinding effect of the glare, I discovered the source of his now obvious pride. I found myself surrounded by innumerable bookshelves built onto the walls of the small room, each tier full of volumes and documents. I saw engravings from another, remote era, each one showing a multitude of mellifluous faces framed by heavily powdered wigs, or crowds of ragged individuals menacingly hoisting rakes and muskets in the streets of a black and white Paris, shabbily drawn by the engraver. I saw names and slogans in the margins, dates and descriptions of what was portrayed, expressions of horror or indifference, dazzled eyes, clawing hands, barrels spilling their contents in the streets, loose cobblestones, columns of smoke, the guillotine. To complete my bewilderment, I saw a painting propped against the wall, its frame badly splattered, and the colors dulled and tarnished over time. Against a chiaroscuro background, at the center of the canvas a face emerged whose features inevitably reflected those of my host with his vivacious, always vigilant eyes, his ruddy complexion and permanently smiling, cordial lips lightly traced with irony, all of this discernible in the portrait that dominated one of the walls.

"You recognize him, don't you?" asked my host after seeing my eyes dart back and forth from the portrait to his face, "He was my great-great-grandfather. He was guillotined in 1793, 'year I' of the Revolution."

Fascinated, I realized that the odor of fish had faded away

around us, substituted by the more tolerable aroma of old paper, leather and bookshelves.

***

If I make a dent in history, gain credit as a humble, unambitious chronicler, it's all due to the man who cleans fish in a stinking shop on Rue Tolbiac. Thanks to him I own a copy of the most trustworthy testimony about the honorable Preceptor Dufeu: his concise, straight, literary testament written behind the Conciergerie's bars while he waited for his turn at the guillotine. It is dated "Thermidor 7" (July 25), the eve of his execution and its credibility is undeniable. A man in disgrace who knows the gallows awaits him doesn't lie when he writes to no one in particular. There is no need for it. I shall now transcribe, literally, those lines scribbled among the lice and other unpleasantness of the prison with that paradoxical mixture of clamor and serenity, of furious conformity that precedes a last stroll through Paris on the way to the guillotine. Some remote cell mate had the good fortune of being acquitted and later thoughtfully remitted the document to the few heirs of the Preceptor. Nobody dared destroy it. As time went by, it finally came to rest in the back room of the shop at Rue Tolbiac, where I had the opportunity to read it. I shall be silent now. It is time to hear the voice of ancestor Dufeu.

Thermidor 7 of Year I

One tiger is no more kind or unpleasant than another. A stone, a tree obviously can't be different from others of their own species. We accept this without objection in the surrounding world—nothing is better or worse than the rest—unless the tiger that comes across our path is hungry, or unless the stone is thrown at us with treacherous intent. The universe around us is unaware of its consequences. Evil, like good manners, is uniquely ascribed to us featherless, rational bipeds. The result of which is—oh! comforting paradox—that all morality is a supreme gesture of volunteerism, an optional fallacy, an avoidable network of good and bad reasons. At present I have been tried and condemned "for acts and attitudes contrary to civic morality." Those who in the past called themselves my comrades, those who with me wrote the words "liberty, equality, fraternity," now cling to an intangible code of ethics, to the transitory dispositions of a flawed Committee of Public Salvation intent on suppressing the indecency of my actions, on evicting me without honor from the face of the earth. All right, on this last night I forgive them for the imminent attack on my cervicals. At the bottom of the bloodied bucket next to the guillotine, my face shall keep a smile, the last expression of an unremorseful man.

Martine sobs in the adjoining cell. Between the bars that separate our cells, I look at her small body, her dark, soft skin, her shy contorted features. In spite of the prison bars, together we have prepared ourselves for this night of tears and unspeakable farewells. When they brought me here a few weeks ago, she was already in the adjoining cell. We talked extensively from the first night, while the other prisoners snored or raved in their sleep, refuting even in the realm of dreams their destiny as condemned to death. Martine speaks a gurgling and jumbled Antillean French, with the faded rr's and the vague flavor of her ancestry, her Matabele grandfather from the village in the African forest. I tell her about social contracts, hermeneutics and issues of state. She doesn't understand a thing I'm saying, but I can't conceive either that the universe exists by the power and will of the Matabele gods. None of all this is important by night when she gets close to the bars and lifts her skirts. The incomparable voluptuousness of her dark thighs presses against the bars; the purple fold of her crotch tenderly hits my eyes in the foul darkness of the dungeon. She invites me to get near and touch with my index finger its damp borders, freely, to feel the warmth of a wound that tries to heal. It shudders at the touch of my fingers, it mumbles like an untamed sparrow at dawn in this last, bleeding summer that finds us in two adjoining cells at the Conciergerie. I later place my fingers on my lips and taste the salty proof of her desire. I smell the hot flow that impregnates my hand and I know, only now, that I'm a noble animal facing death, neither better nor worse than others, now free of the Encyclopedia and the grotesque, irrelevant threats of my former comrades. Was it Hobbes who said that man is a wolf toward man? How foolish! Martine dispels such a concept with a vengeance the instant I free my virile instrument from its velvety cell, the precise instant in which I unbutton my fly and encourage the animal to breathe the jail's unhealthy air, coax him to find his way through the bars and finally get close to Martine's warm, damp cleft. The instant I hear her moan on the other side we turn into two crouching felines, caught in feverish swinging motion, forward and backward, shamelessly open, separated by bars no longer real, giving in to moans and sighs, our hearts beating wildly while we hold on to the cell's bars. At the precise moment that I let myself go into her womb, somebody grumbles gibberish in a corner of the cell, while we both confirm that no barrier of iron can keep us apart. At my age, having crossed over the threshold of 40, devoured by her glossy buttocks, I finally discover love and feel the deepest sorrow for her quiet weeping in the adjoining cell.

Yes, I have behaved shamelessly in public, I'm not afraid to confess it now. I have displayed in the streets all the attributes that most, Robespierre himself included, keep under wraps, hypocritically reserving their view to the privacy of the connubial bedroom. I opted for straightforwardness early in life, during adolescence, when I started my reflections on public matters. Machiavelli taught me not to dilute good motives in jumbled verbosity. With Rousseau I learned to appreciate good manners and tolerance. My German governess, voluptuous and more direct than Machiavelli, once enveloped my private animal with her hands. In this last night at the Conciergerie, my memory only retains Frau Emma's reaction. It was to her that I showed, for the first time, my naked rump, turning my back to her and letting my trousers slide down when she was reciting some verses of Petrarch to me. My governess didn't understand me. Nobody ever would. I know that my buttocks are thin and flaccid, but there was no excuse for the slap on the face with which I was punished, along with the stern order to pull up my pants.

This experience failed to discourage me. Years later, a short distance from a young ladies' school in Toulon, I waited for the girls to pour onto the street with the perfume and wild, free manners of adolescence. Then I slipped my hands into my waistband, turned my back to that multitude of young hearts and again let my trousers fall. It was a mild noon in Toulon. The sun lovingly touched my exposed backside. I didn't get to see my adolescent audience, their expressions of surprise and bewilderment...I only remember that a vast silence fell on the street, followed by some exclamations, guffaws and outraged warnings. "Look...he is naked!"—more laughter, catcalls and whispers. I cared little for the girls' reactions. I wasn't aiming to test the ignoble signs of fear and rejection in their diaphanous, young faces. Now I know: that day in Toulon I achieved happiness. Rousseau's thought (Man in his natural state is good) had just literally become incarnate in my actions. Happy, fulfilled, invincible...until somebody notified the authorities responsible for public order and I found myself surrounded by several uniformed public servants, grabbed by the neck and thrown face down on the stone pavement in the midst of adolescent shrieks and diverse admonitions. "Get dressed, jerk...pervert!" they shouted while two of my captors tried desperately to raise my trousers. It wasn't any more humiliating or painful than my governess' slap on the face. From then on, punishment would be a required factor for the fulfillment of my endeavors. Pleasure would always call for a hand ready to strike me, someone waiting to twist my arm or throw me to the ground.

That day in Toulon—I was nearly thirty and responsible for my actions—I was taken to the local police station. The highest ranking officer took charge of my interrogation. There was no additional violence or degrading incident. Until then my clothes had been of the best quality. My last name linked me to the wealthiest merchants in the region. Having left behind the streets and the young ladies, I was treated with respect, with that servile deference that the guardians of public order displayed before the Revolution toward members of the nobility.

"Let's see, Monsieur Dufeu," the officer in charge of the questioning said with some sarcasm, "why have you done such a thing?"

I answered without hesitation:

"Close to that school there are several carriages drawn by horses. If I remember correctly, they all go around naked. They should also be brought in here for interrogation. I refuse to explain the reasons for my behavior unless it's in the presence of those animals. Man also is born and dies in slavery, Commissioner, but when the law is dispensed with equality, it's not hard…"

It's no surprise that I was judged somewhat deranged and set free after a brief admonition that I shall omit for being inane. I have said this before: no moral consideration affects, in its objectives and usefulness, one who holds it precariously. No sacred principle—I'm now convinced—can save those who believe in it. The Toulon Commissioner has already preceded me to the guillotine. And the horses in Toulon probably still run naked through the city's streets.

I continued my foolishness in the streets and environs of my native port city for some years with no different results. One spring day I went near the wharves, at the time of day when the poverty stricken of every sort gathered to load and unload the cargo. Without thinking twice, I got on top of a bale of hay, turned my back to all those people and once more let my trousers down, yelling, "Rise in arms, my dispossessed comrades, our time is near!" No doubt it wasn't a favorable occasion for demonstrations and harangues of that nature. A mass of cabbages and tomatoes as well as unflattering qualifiers and epithets contributed once more to my disappointment. I wasted no time in jumping to the boards of the wharf, hurriedly pulling up my trousers just as cabbages and tomatoes were substituted with stones. I knew already that the days of the monarchy were numbered. In Toulon, in Marseilles, in the whole area of the Midi, beggars and laborers were giving out sure signs of their legitimate resentment. The pristine behind of nobility was about to get the most colossal kick that anybody had ever addressed to it. The contempt shown toward my own unimportant hindquarters was only the prelude to that final boot.

In the fields surrounding the city, I harassed the sound-minded landowners, merchants, their wives and offspring a couple of times. The police and the royal guard invariably took it upon themselves to discourage me. As expected, I soon acquired abominable fame as a pervert and exhibitionist. Such reputation was occasionally ratified by sharp shoves and skillfully hurled stones, spit and insults, a beating with clubs, and attempted lynching that I miraculously avoided by making good use of my oratorical powers. I reiterated once more my argument about the obvious impunity of horses' nudity in the streets of Toulon. I knew then and still consider myself righteous and without blame. Buonarroti had to cover God Himself with hypocritical strokes of paint in the Sistine Chapel. Why should the mob from a port lost in the South of France be less drastic when confronted with my posterior? I now call on the great Michelangelo, and the metaphor is certainly meaningful. Upon releasing my belt and dropping my pants down my legs, I became Buonarroti's God, supreme and omniscient, unchallenged in his power and his sacred nudity, indifferent to the improvised audience that successively included Frau Emma, the young students, stevedores and noblemen of Toulon—all the indignant archangels who, unexpectedly, witnessed the impudent unveiling of my behind. As far as I modestly knew, at the time there was no greater pleasure than to find myself suddenly naked in front of a crowd, nude and irrepressible on a splendid evening in Toulon, and then to suffer the humiliation followed by defeat under the always inconsequential pelting of stones. "A new era is dawning," I would think. "Stripped of all textile contrivance, free of the obsolete monarchic morality, we shall find again the way to paradise, finally we will be absolved, we may drink innocently from its streams and ponds, together we shall eat its fruits, naked and immaculate…"

In the winter of '63 the situation in our overseas possessions became indefensible. The crown could not hold back the American rebels: all of Louisiana and most of Quebec had to be abandoned by Louis XVI's imperial armies. Cities and fields were full of frustrated colonists who returned empty-handed speaking about equality, teaching laborers and peasants the ideas of the American independents. Fear suffused the court and the palaces, and the nobles' wigs looked more powdered and offensive than ever. Without wasting time I went to Paris.

There I met Danton, Saint-Just, Robespierre and the eccentric Talleyrand, a fine courtier who now lives in a foreign country and will probably outlive us all. Without batting an eye, as soon as we were introduced he said to me: "My dear Dufeu, man was granted the gift of speech to hide his thoughts." He may be right. He is one of the few who until now has avoided the hygienic efficiency of the Committee of Public Salvation. In any case, I detest his attitudes. I have never hidden my ideas and half my fellows, or slightly less, are acquainted with the lower part of my body, my forthright, undaunted rump.

Together with the best brains of my generation, I contributed to our citizens' uprising until we led Louis XVI to the guillotine only a few months ago. In the heat of the riots and within the taverns by the Seine, I wrote my fundamental text, "On Morality and Sound Judgment in the Management of Human Societies," which many consider a pale reflection of ideas already expounded by Rousseau. I couldn't care less about such opinions. I have drunk fully from the fountain of the old Genevan master, but I differ from him in that each of my statements is based on pragmatic motives, on the blood and sweat that have already flowed through France's streets. I have, of course, talked about tolerance, social pacts and agreements. I was the object of many beatings and punishments, tangible manifestations of intolerance, when for the hundredth time I exhibited my behind at the "Jardin des Plantes" or in the vicinity of the Tuileries. Anticipating the Jacobin's purifying activities, I also conceived the beginnings of a new era, a new world that takes us back to Genesis. Robespierre and his followers have proclaimed this the "Year I," yet this is nothing but a formal disguise, a clever contrivance designed to hide their bloody hands. Only I have dared walk naked through Paris. Only I, Martine and the toothless, anonymous wretches who share this cell with me, have been violently expelled from their false paradise with the imminent complicity of a sheet of sharp metal.

It would be too long a list to enumerate my disagreements with the Committee's hounds. Suffice it to say that Robespierre's patience toward my suggestions apparently came to an end in early spring, while he still considered me one of his favorite advisers. During a regular meeting in his office where I listened to his exhausting, moralizing tirades I decided I'd had enough, that this should stop. And retiring into a corner of his large office, I let my trousers slide down my legs with deliberate slowness. I suspect that at this precise moment Maximilien de Robespierre realized at last the infinite distance that separated me from his thinking. We had never been real friends. He accuses me now of being vain and explosive. I know that he is a puritan afflicted with weakness of character. He is less impetuous than I, but more cunning. He now holds the reins of government, intent on solving old tavern disputes with the help of Dr. Guillotin's awesome invention.

Ominous winds of sorrow blow for Parisians. It is "Year I" and it is not exactly the Garden of Eden. A little over a month ago I was unceremoniously abducted from my home to appear before the Committee to which I had to explain my bottom's characteristics and its too frequent displays in the streets of Paris. My books and writings have been burned as a strange act of exorcism that, paradoxically, takes us back to our enemies in the Inquisition. I have nothing left but this minimal amount of paper and a pen that our compassionate and congenial jailer has reserved for my last statements. I have nothing left but the unshakable dignity of my purposes, the certainty that I need not justify my actions. I didn't apologize to the Committee! My attorney, a clown who the court appointed for my defense, called on disgraceful excuses of a lesser kind during his intervention. In the darkness of the room, in the midst of the vociferous reaction of the pack that witnessed my public degradation, I heard facetious references to the unbridled passion of youth, a quaint praise of my behind, some peculiar considerations about the well established usefulness of this part of our anatomy and other similar foolishness. But there was not one mention of my writings, my steadfast loyalty to the Revolution nor to the Jacobins and their depredations. The trial ended with the reading of the sentence and the final invitation from the sorry bird presiding at the tribunal for my last pronouncement. I remembered my adolescence in Toulon. I remembered the chief of police's questioning, and once more I answered without hesitation.

"The horses in Toulon walk nude in the city's streets and a horse is neither better nor less deserving than others. Except for the fact that you all wear clothes, you are no different from the horses of Toulon, my citizens. May you sleep in peace until your turn comes!"

It's already dawn. Through the bars of the cell's window I can hear, emerging from the somber courtyard of the Conciergerie, voices and the neighing of the animals that will escort me to the scaffold. Martine doesn't sob any more. For hours she has remained by the bars that separate us. She watches me silently while I write these lines, patiently waiting for the last caresses. I have only a few minutes left. It's time to taste the fruit for the last time. For the last time I unbuckle my belt, let my trousers slide to my ankles, uncover my body before Martine and I see no sign of shock in her black eyes. For the last time I feel like a free citizen of Paris, now in this last dawn of my life.

Long live the Revolution!

M.S. Dufeu

There were no other annotations on the manuscript. Everything ended there, serenely, with the dry affirmation of his revolutionary loyalty. Utterly fascinated, I finished the first reading in the back room of the fish shop, under the impatient vigilance of the remote descendant of Dufeu at the Rue Tolbiac.

"Is this authentic?" I asked, struggling to return to the present.

"It is," he stated decisively.

By the waning light in the room, I examined his face again, the obvious resemblance of his features with those of the portrait against the wall. Practically everything was identical, except the hair. My host's was black and curly, as it probably was, still, in the Matabele tribes and other African villages.

"You can confirm the dates and details of the trial in the municipal archives," he added.

I did so the very next day. Every repressive and punitive regime professes a strange addiction to reports, the morbid desire to attest to the spilling of blood with official papers and seals. Adhering strictly to this principle, the old compilation of documents bequeathed by the Jacobin tribunals to the archives of Paris offered a fairly detailed description of the trials and executions that characterized their meager prestige. A report dated "9 Thermidor Year I" relates "the accusation of the people of France against Maurice Sebastien Dufeu, guilty of violating public morality," and describes the trial. The more extensive description by the official reporter was about the execution itself and the last gesture of the prisoner facing the crowd, at the precise moment that the blade was leaving the upper part of the structure. At that exact instant the notorious Preceptor Defeu decided to play his trump card and with assumed dignity, kneeling on the scaffold, his head already clamped in the stocks, he let fall—now certainly for the last time—his velvet trousers before the executioner and his spectators.

***

I couldn't help but return to the fish shop a week later. I found only the red-haired assistant behind the counter.

"Monsieur Defeu is not well at all," he explained yawning. "He didn't show up for a few days, then yesterday his wife called to tell me that he had been found walking around the 'Jardin des Plantes' without his trousers. Incredible, eh?"

Badly shaken, I glanced at the showcases full of dying crustaceans, some of them still bitterly waving their claws.

"Do you want some oysters today, Monsieur?"

the last supper

Some years ago he had been an active member of the Amsterdam diocese, a fact that in itself justified his story and tribulations. In any case it was a minor tragedy, with gastronomic and religious overtones. Fear had made him stray from the church and the gospel, the same reason that makes others persevere. He shared his story with us, gladly although nervously, at a symposium on ethnology that Laura and I attended to expound on some foolishness such as the cooking techniques of the Zulus or the courtship customs of the Mobutu in subequatorial Africa. His last name was Van der Veer, tall, blond, muscular, handsome. He might have been 35 years old. He wore eyeglasses and already sported a deeply receding hairline at the forehead beside his permanently furrowed brow. At an early age he had graduated with a degree in anthropology and linguistic theory at Louvain. He was fluent in Spanish, spoke some Italian and a smattering of German.

"And the Maquenda language," he added when we were introducing ourselves.

"What is that?" asked Laura.

"The dialect of an Amazonian tribe," he explained. "I'll be speaking about it later."

It seems to me that in his own reserved way he felt attracted to Laura, who in her own reserved way also felt drawn to him. Perhaps I should have distanced myself from the symposium one morning to let them define their feelings. Or they may have found a definition without my having to leave the symposium.

At later encounters he went into details of his life. He decided to confess to us, in the cafeteria, the reason for his tormented brow: the promised story of Amazonia. Following his family tradition, after graduating at Louvain and returning to his country, he joined the militant ranks of his church in the streets of Amsterdam. His adherence to the local campaign was well thought out, according to his confession by the second shot of whisky. Through that conduit he hoped to join—as it actually happened—one of the missions that his diocese used to send to the Third World and other God forsaken latitudes.

Before his wish was fulfilled he had to wait, be patient and teach linguistics at some college in Amsterdam. To gain the respect of his ministers he tirelessly traveled through the city on his bicycle, getting lost among the canals and edifices of the urban suburbs, knocking on every immigrant's door to offer his church's publications to whoever showed up at the threshold. Laura and I felt vaguely comforted by the thought that those things could also happen to a Louvain Ph.D.

His story smacked slightly of a certain irony that revealed his gradual estrangement from the gospels. Something, maybe the youthful, tiresome plodding along the streets of Amsterdam, had irredeemably worn down his faith, leaving just shreds of it, a poor semblance of his initial fervor, preceding the stage when everything would turn into a handful of sand slipping through his fingers, before the resentment and the mockery. Before fear set in.

The symposium was about to end when we finally discovered his intimate motivations (which he seemed eager to exorcize into the ears of a third party). The motivations that had turned him into a missionary in reverse, the man who now proclaimed the advantages of agnosticism, "the pitfalls of faith..."

"It's better not to count on God," he repeated once the third whisky had saturated his brain. "Better leave Him to take care of airplanes, particularly in stormy weather!"

One day his ministers had summoned him to the diocese to report that they had approved his request to be assigned to one of the new missions that the church was planning to send to the Third World. Van der Veer thought of Africa or Southeast Asia. The assignment was far more exotic. Its purpose was to establish contact with the Maquenda tribe, an Amazonian community recently discovered in the jungle by Schumacher. Remotely related to the Chamacocos and the Guaranís, they numbered little more than 200, which placed them at a critical level, close to extinction. They walked around naked and built huts with no walls, just a roof of leaves supported by four wood posts. They ate certain local animals, fish, roots, manioc bread and fruits, although there were references in the tribe's carved stones about ancient cannibalistic habits that were no longer practiced. Nevertheless, they were friendly and welcomed the white man, as Schumacher had confirmed during his brief one-week stay to open the way for the missions from Amsterdam.

It was now a matter of getting there, Bible in hand, to instruct them about the Gospels, the word of God, without going against their traditions, which included indiscriminate sex and barbecued monkey. That was why the diocese picked Van der Veer, who would know how to mix faith and reason in the bewildering reaches of the Mato Grosso.

On a Friday in March they boarded the KLM jet with one stop in Recife: Van der Veer and another four expeditionaries, among them a physician, a botanist and two archeologists, all of them members of the church. From Recife they continued the flight on a biplane to Belem and then to Manaos, the last population center of importance before entering the jungle by the river, for all five of them to be swallowed by the sun's beams, the thunderous rain and the mosquitoes. They navigated for two days in a western direction on the Solimoes, a branch of the Amazon that leads to the thick of the rain forest and the Maquenda territory. At night they camped on the river's bank. The outboard motor functioned steadily, keeping the caimans at bay. The native who handled the boat and took the helm, Salgado by name, had no idea that the Maquenda existed. On the third day they divined their territory on the right bank of the river, seeing about twenty faces among the trees. Salgado reluctantly brought the boat to shore, hurriedly took leave of his passengers and headed back to Manaos with the Solimoes current now favoring his progress.

Seconds later the Maquenda approached the missionaries, marveling at their height, at the smoking pipe between Hoelzel's lips, the blond and red beards, chattering their conclusions, laughing at any insignificant thing such as the muddy shoes or

Renner's wristwatch. Van der Veer himself made clear the essential purpose of the visit from the very beginning by uncovering the small crucifix they carried, a red-daubed, realistic carving of Christ, pale and dying, the thorn crown on his forehead, his flesh pierced by nails.

The Maquenda, men, women and children, recoiled in shock.

"Jesus," said Van der Veer in Dutch. "The Son of God."

***

They set up camp a short distance from the Maquenda village. Several days elapsed before the members of the tribe decided to approach the crucifix. Hoelzel had placed it vertically on top of a rock near the camping tents, in a suitable crack in the stone. The first one to break the reverential aura that surrounded the statuette, to examine it, to sniff and touch it, was a heavyset and cheerful individual that the rest of the tribe called Aye-Maké. Satisfied with his inspection of the crucifix, Aye-Maké clearly expressed his approval to the five missionaries by smiling widely and bowing many times before leading his companions back to the village.

He was the tribe's cook, to whom the rest of the villagers provided Amazonian fishes, monkeys and parrots killed with their blowguns. They also gave him large amounts of herbs to prepare the daily meals, a select gastronomic display of roasted meats and spices marinated in vegetal extracts.

"These people practiced cannibalism in the past, isn't that true?" Hoelzel asked Van der Veer one moonlit night when all five gathered around the fire.

"That was a long time ago, too long ago" replied Van der Veer in a paternal and reassuring tone.

"Today they have nothing left but the iconography," added Renner, one of the archeologists. "Only yesterday I was examining the petroglyphs. That German who discovered these people was right, he interpreted them correctly."

"What petroglyphs?"

"In the village. A polished stone with centuries-old incisions. The past of the tribe."

"And what's on it?"

"Men," expounded Renner. "Armed with clubs and spears, and others in horizontal positions. Over the fire, well seasoned for sure, like the delicatessen that Aye-Maké prepares for us."

"How many centuries since that happened?"

"Several," Van der Veer reiterated. "Now they prefer monkey."

By the end of a couple of weeks they were able to decipher some of the fundamental elements of the Maquenda vocabulary, and they started the task of evangelization by giving the natives rudimentary explanations of Genesis, the Ten Commandments, Christ's grievous path to the cross. In the evenings they had collective readings of the Bible sitting by the small crucifix stuck in the rock, which the Maquenda gazed at as if mesmerized, without taking their eyes off the wounds. Van der Veer interpreted this as a good sign.

A month after their arrival at the village, Hoelzel reminded his companions about vaccines that should by now be waiting for them to pick up in Manaos. Somebody must fetch them by way of the river in one of the indigenous canoes. Nobody wanted to leave the village. They drew lots and Van der Veer was the loser, pulling out the shortest twig.

"The return voyage was far briefer, thanks to the Solimoes' favorable current" he explained now in the cafeteria. "I arrived in Manaos twenty-four hours later. I recovered there from the aboriginal food and the mosquitoes. The vaccines arrived a couple of days later packed in protective material. The third day at dawn I started back with Salgado, who demanded almost twice the original fee.

"What a character!" remarked Laura.

Van der Veer kept silent. We waited in vain for him to wrap up his story. His unexpected silence went on until he yawned, took a look at his watch and stood up on the pretext of having to return to his hotel in order to prepare his next day's report.

"But what happened with the Maquendas?" asked Laura, disappointed.

"Tomorrow," he said with a theatrical air and walked towards the exit. "We shall meet right here at the bar, if it's all right with you."

"What a character!" Laura insisted. "You wouldn't leave us in suspense until tomorrow?"

"That's exactly what I'm going to do," he said, then threw her a kiss from the door of the bar.

Laura remained disgruntled for longer than expected.

The next evening our doubts were dispelled at the hotel bar. We had an early dinner, but all three of us stayed at the bar until past midnight. Van der Veer imbibed an excess of brandy while searching for the appropriate moment to tell us about his unforgettable return to the Maquenda village. With less weight on board—this time only Salgado and himself were the passenger and crew—they reached their destination in half the time, but the reception was different. He was hoping to see Hoelzel smoking his pipe by the riverbank. Or Renner. Not even the Indian faces were to be seen among the trees like the first time. Salgado preferred to wait for him on board, until he confirmed that everything was all right.

Uneasy, he walked to the place where they had set up their camping tents, but he found them empty. Only the crucifix stuck in the boulder suggested their presence. He assumed that his companions were all in the village, probably gathered for a catechism session with the aborigines. Yet his instinct told him to seek cover in the vegetation, so as to get near without being seen.

From the thicket he saw them: the whole tribe assembled around the fire and the chef, Aye-Maké, his back to the river, wielding a knife. In the background were Hoelzel, Renner and the other two, each nailed to a cross, their bodies limp, already dead. Properly seasoned for dinner and the always avid palate of the Maquenda.

"They had reverted to their ancestral diet," explained our friend. "With the help of our sacred cookbook."

From July on, the heat increased and the trail of ants spread to other places in the kitchen. Shortly afterward I gave up on the Hamilton translation and his obsession for mitogenic radiation, which I don't share. I don't regret my desertion. No slave recently escaped from the cotton fields abhors his initiative under the star-studded night, delighting in the wild, though transitory, scent of his fragile freedom.

Beginning in August, I went down to the square with the little money I had left, joining the pigeons that swarmed around the fountain and the flabby old men on the benches, or the North African immigrants whose manifest destiny seemed to be the constant avoidance of police harassment.

That day I saw them for the first time on the adjoining bench. A ragged group of three or four individuals, worn out, deep shadows under the eyes. She was in the middle, a still young woman passing a bottle between them (some wine of scant bouquet). They looked like a troupe of primates delousing under the summer sun, silently, with no reproaches, intent on the shared ceremonial.

They didn't refuse me a sip, that day or the next. I'm now one of them, although I don't know their names. Sometimes we fight over a bottle, sometimes over even less than that.

The last thing I heard about Cerutti was that he had died (which in all truth is the last thing we hear about anybody). In Africa, or more precisely, in Kangala, a difficult country to locate and still harder to pronounce, with the recent trend among correspondents and diplomats to translate everything back to Swahili and other native languages. I knew that country by personal experience, and Malabo, the capital; I ran into Cerutti there in late '82. But Africa was only the backdrop for all that developed behind the scenes, and our encounter was like one of those brief, purposeless meetings in a public restroom, when someone we knew in childhood suddenly finds us with our instrument in our hand and starts asking questions about our family while we hurry to self-consciously rid ourselves of our minor fluids. His death (Cerutti's), mentioned without honors in the international section of *Le Monde*, made me think of him as he was in university days, although the sequence of his unstable life ran rather in the opposite direction: from university to the savanna, then to the teletypes and then the report in *Le Monde*, with a photo of his body stretched out in a room at the Malabo Palace on the day Mokoena's victorious troops entered the capital to establish socialism, or whatever it was, in the Soviet or Chinese style, depending on which side Mokoena was leaning to at the time.

We had met before at the university on the occasion of some multitudinous assembly at a time of tear gas and wild street demonstrations. I remember getting along well with him from the start. We felt attuned in sharing a secret rejection of party rhetoric and slogans. There was talk about a revolution that would break out across the continent—so they said—starting in the altiplano and from there spreading down the Andean massif to surrounding areas, including Santiago, Buenos Aires, São

Paulo, all the important urban centers, more or less as Guevara postulated. Cerutti dismissed such an ambitious project with deliberate irony. He wanted to know the name of the leader (the man who would guide the people down from the altiplano), how many guns were available, and where the capital of the new socialist republic would be, so as to enact the traditional, triumphant march into the city. I kept quiet, forecasting through my silence the lukewarm state of my future commitment, that gradual, sneaky affinity of almost all youthful Bolsheviks toward the premises of the established order. I suppose that inwardly I shared the calculated glibness of the old Churchill, to whom democracy—democracy in his own style—was the only guarantee that a 5:00 A.M. knock on the door would be the initiative of the milkman and not some mastodon, gun in hand.

Cerutti and I were strangers to urban life. He came from the Argentine pampas—he liked to surround himself with an air of mystery, like the gaucho who has left behind the age of the bolas. I also came from the south, from the neighboring country, where nobody demands that one hurry and life goes on mostly under a roof, with a curtain of rain at the window, beyond which there is nothing except the mud, some ramshackle dwellings, and hens and cows numb from the cold. His was a damp pampa; it rained too in his childhood memories.

Along with some other nostalgics from the provinces, we lived in a boarding house near the university. It was far from paradise, due in part to the monotony of the menu. We ate plenty of cabbage, with soup or spaghetti on alternate days. Cerutti sat at the head of the table, in deep silence, head bowed, hands folded in front of his plate, in an almost reverent attitude. The rest of us watched out of the corners of our eyes, fascinated by his gestures.

"Well," he would finally say, emerging from silence and meditative remoteness. "Let's stir it up, guys. We have to stir things up."

And he would pierce pasta, sauce and cheese with his fork, and twirl it solemnly, like a deposed prince brought down to the gutter, intent on regaining the privileges of his position under the humblest of circumstances, even when ingesting a dish of noodles. The rest of us watched the enactment of this ceremony. We twirled as he did and felt as one with his movements, as though we belonged to something, even if it was just that meal, our peculiar version of the last supper. In his own way, he was a collective spokesman, although several among the diners— indifferent to his influence—would start to gulp their spaghetti, ignoring the ritual. It is well known that misfortune leads to voraciousness, whenever indulgence is possible.

Our friendship in the shelter of the underground didn't last long. The people's uprising was taking its time, and alliances without a clear direction do not prosper. Every potential rebel in the area, the few that survived, eventually deserted to work at a bank or a government agency, under the pretext of "infiltrating" the system and weakening it from within, unaware that the system had the same intention toward them. I vaguely remember Cerutti getting himself expelled from the university after making some comment in public about the rector's mother, and returning to Argentina. In the days before his departure, we drank quantities of *mate* in the backyard of the boarding house, where a grimy hammock surviving from times immemorial hung beneath the Southern Cross. The murmur of water boiling for coffee or *mate* was like a subterfuge and prelude for our talks, which lasted until two or three in the morning, sometimes even later, when nothing was left around us but silence, an occasional distant siren and the oppression of idle hours.

"This thing isn't working, man," he concluded on one of those evenings, pensive, stretched out in the hammock, belly and hairs showing under his shirt. "These people waste their time in meetings, discussing sanction proposals. What with party discipline and the ones obliterated by the government's pack of hounds, we won't have any militants left. This is what happens when the Inquisition prevails, man, it's always the same. Everyone lights their own little bonfire!"

"And so what are you going to do?"

"About what?"

"About the party, the struggle...all that crap."

"I'm shoving off from this place as soon as possible. That's what I have the pampas for."

"And the cows," I added.

"Exactly. An Argentinean without cows around is like a dog without fleas, you know that. Another *mate*, man? You must stir it well."

Several months later he sent me a postcard from his new location. He was sick of cows, prairies, gauchos and barbecues. He was up to his ears in pampas, yet he gave no details about these wonders. He was heading for Paris, "where being an Argentinean is always an advantage, and from there to Africa, where the blacks have just gotten rid of the last European colonials. Must be seen to be believed, man."

2

The weekend following his death, *L'Humanité* published a page-and-a-half report in its Sunday news summary. Not about Cerutti, who meant little to anyone, but to honor Mokoena, the new man in charge of the country. In the article he spoke of international credit and austerity, although it was hard to imagine greater austerity than the people of Kangala had already been practicing, at least at the gastronomic level.

The author of the article, a correspondent for one of the government agencies, did include an inset which mentioned Cerutti, the Argentinean mysteriously assassinated at the Malabo Palace. The text ended: "Malabo police have been unable to assign responsibility to anyone in the death of the Argentinean citizen found under suspicious circumstances in the most expensive suite of the Malabo Palace on the same day that the rebel army entered the capital, while government officials hastened to eliminate proof of their shady deals in the ministries of the old regime, and the deposed leader, Moses Rashola, started his journey to exile, or the savanna—most probably to exile, considering his hefty bank accounts in European institutions."

The dead man, in shirtsleeves ("...of fine Italian silk, obviously expensive, bought in a shop for foreigners"), displayed a bullet hole in his chest and an exit wound in his back. According to the correspondent's report, the bullet had lodged in the mattress. It was of heavy caliber, the kind of projectile used by guerrillas from every fighting faction. The distribution of homogeneous weapons among opposing parties put a strain on the local police investigation. Could the killing have been perpetrated by the winning faction? Or by the vanquished, possibly motivated by grudges whose nature remained in the shadows? This basic uncertainty led to other questions. What was an Argentinean citizen doing in Malabo on the day of the victory with an expired passport and dressed in the highest quality clothes just bought at Barney's, the British colony's favorite store? Could this case involve espionage? Or possibly a political crime? The police commissioner assigned to the case didn't seem particularly eager to solve it. Mokoena's victorious troops were intent on reorganizing the police cadres of the tyrant Rashola across the board. The commissioner's main concern now was to save his position (that is, if he managed to save his own neck). As for the Argentinean, the sooner they buried him under several meters of dirt, the better.

But it was impossible to bury him. A week later, a cable from Malabo reported that somebody stole his corpse from the morgue where it had been stored. "It's not the first Argentinean to disappear these days," the consul of Argentina in the capital of Kangala commented to Agence France Press. Nobody could tell if this remark was a cruel joke or a dig at unscrupulous officers in uniform. The brief report for the first time included a picture of Cerutti after death. A maid at the hotel had found him on Saturday, Victory Day, around noon, when she entered the suite to make the bed and clean up the room, just after the rebel troops had marched past the hotel. He was lying spread-eagled across the sheets, still warm, she told the *Gazette de Kangala*. I read the story, and looked at the picture of Cerutti spreadeagled over the sheets while I was having an evening drink on the terrace of the Estoril in Paris. The camera had caught him from the chest up. His face, now emaciated, his eyes half closed, fixed on some distant object, the detail of his slightly open lips, the scraggly beard, sunken cheeks, deep shadows under the eyes, a certain air of nobility—managed to utterly upset me there on the Estoril terrace. In its way, the myth returned. He looked like a recent version, although less solemn, of Guevara in the mountains of Bolivia.

3

I remember the day he arrived at our hut, sometime around the year '82. I lived with Theresa on the outskirts of Malabo by a river that was no more, to whose dusty bed, sucked dry by the drought, local flamingoes and ostriches flocked in frustration. He had put on weight. I became aware of it when I saw him climbing with great difficulty on the rocky trail that led to the river (not a river anymore), on his way from the nameless settlement where Theresa and I bought kerosene for our lamps, local bread and the canned goods brought in from Malabo to provide food for the Protestant missionaries from Brighton scattered throughout the region, meaning the whole rather insignificant country.

Cerutti then became something more significant for me. With a conspicuous belly, open *guayabera* shirt, a greasy handkerchief around his neck, muddy shoes, slacks long ago white but no more, and untrimmed beard, he dragged a trunk on unreliable wheels. He came from Nigeria, which he had left four or five months earlier, advancing through four or five essentially similar countries full of tall and bony guerrillas wearing berets and rope sandals, regular soldiers reluctantly patrolling the vicinity of a meaningless border, women carrying jars of water on their heads, babies with swollen bellies, grumpy oxen, snakes and flies.

We greeted each other soberly. We both had known we'd meet again. Perhaps we brought it about without even trying, in order to talk of rains and foolish provincial trivia in the midst of the tremendous African drought. He brought with him a supply of *mate*. On the third day of sucking on an aluminum straw, I felt a doubt.

"How did you find me?" I asked.

He thought for a minute.

"There are no secrets in Africa."

On the fourth day Theresa joined the conversation, crouching nonchalantly by the fire where the mosquitoes harassed her shiny brown skin, well fed by the charitable deeds of Protestant missionaries from Brighton. She walked through life wearing only a loincloth. This exacerbated Cerutti's loneliness.

"Man, that kid...," he said suddenly on the fifth day, "she's not bad."

"No."

"To tell you the truth, she looks pretty good."

"*Very* good."

"You won't mind if I offer her a sip of *mate*?"

"No."

Theresa accepted his offer readily, with the delight of a small tamed animal once stolen from the bush and the tribal night. She had been stolen (from the bush and the tribal night) by some British functionary in shorts with a wife devoted to cricket at the local country club, so that Theresa would clear away their china and prepare their evening gin fizz. Thus, she literally came into my hands. Due to the British gin fizz habit, her domestic services had gradually extended to the whole day. This was far from her concept of how to get along with the invader. During a Commonwealth celebration in her master's home, I saw her from the corner of my eye, with her hands hidden under a tray loaded with olives and Scotch. They had dressed her with a small starched apron, through which I sensed her wild voluptuousness. At the end of the gathering, on my way to the bathroom, I met her face to face. Under the spell of my delight in her African body, we contrived some nonsense in pidgin English, and with many smiles drank the remaining Scotch together and proceeded by mutual agreement to abolish slavery.

Some international philanthropic organization had approved one of my projects for the building of a well on the outskirts of Malabo, close to a river that still flowed. Theresa agreed to go with me. As time went by, we forgot about the well, the river dried up and she went back to walking around in a loincloth, which greatly facilitated my losing myself between her shiny thighs, preferably in the evenings. After a short while, we fell into the gin fizz habit of her British master. It turned into a routine with no fixed schedule.

I wasn't pleased about Cerutti preparing her *mates*. She didn't care. Her peculiar cosmogony of wide prairies, volcanoes and antelopes had placed me in the category of a bird-man, or something like it, that had penetrated into her destiny by divine design, with the purpose of returning her to the savanna and her natural surroundings, in this case, the waterless river. Her grandfather—or possibly the tribe's medicine man, I could never clarify this—had predicted this in a revelation coinciding with her first menstruation. She seemed reasonably convinced of all this. Until Cerutti showed up with his trunk, sweating like a pig, squandering *mate* herb throughout the planet. Theresa asked herself if this fat little guy might be the bird-man assigned by prophecy to rescue her, also considering that my funds for the well were beginning to dry up. Like all African women, she was pragmatic.

For the time being, Cerutti's conduct remained well within the bounds of our friendship. Apart from preparing Theresa's *mate*, he didn't even really speak to her. It may have been because of loyalty toward me. Or perhaps because of Theresa's lack of interest in the Boca Juniors soccer team, Perón or the Malvinas. I half listened to him, both of us intoxicated by the aromatic twilights, the distant calls of animals, and the effects of the last of our Ballantine's. I didn't care much about the Boca Juniors either, but the alternative was the litany of stories about nocturnal abductions and psychoanalysts hurled into the South Atlantic waters from helicopters, a subject far less tolerable. Cerutti felt the same way. He had walked out of the Buenos Aires night and its terrors, so he talked about soccer because nothing else was safe, with so many dead that nobody would ever see again. That's why I felt so shocked a couple of years later when I learned, in a brief newspaper report, about the disappearance of his corpse.

By the fire, the African night enveloped us. Theresa had wrapped herself in a blanket, curled up like a feline in the refuge of the elementary function of sleep, free from numbers, theorems, sense of honor, and the rest. Cerutti and I had surrendered to silence, listening to her breathing by the fire, fully awake and waiting for dawn when the sky filled up again with light and rosy tones, iridescent in the distance, while flocks of cranes and flamingoes crossed the sky on their way to other cli*mates*. During that luminous hour it seemed as if the river by our hut would again fill with water. It almost seemed that all our dead might reappear and finally rest in peace.

4

After a week elapsed, I asked him about the trunk.

"What trunk?"

"The one you dragged in."

"Ah! yes! The trunk."

He remained silent for a short while, the straw for the *mate* between his lips, sipping intermittently. He liked to give himself airs by such stalling tricks, like a religious leader meditating on an answer for one of his disciples. It happens occasionally to all of us in our eagerness to be relevant, maybe even to a Secretary of Foreign Affairs or any decadent guru, the kind who keeps silent and meditates before answering some nonsense that his followers will canonize in some cheap paperback. Cerutti enjoyed surrounding himself with such a grandiose halo. Even when he died wrapped in fine Italian silk in a five-star hotel, there was something about him akin to a symphonic tango. He smelled refined and wealthy, although—as in the tango—the slums, the countryside and the cows lurked in the background.

"What do you have in there?" I insisted, pointing at the trunk now lying against the side of the hut.

"Uniforms," he replied.

"What sort of uniforms?"

"For the guerrilla army."

"The guerrillas? Which ones?"

"Whoever. The ones that are ahead. Or perhaps the losers, to comfort them. Preferably the ones that pay cash. It's the law of supply and demand, man. Don't look at me like that."

"Where did you get them?"

"British Navy surplus. They gave me the shirts at half price and threw the pants in for free."

"And the rest?"

"There's a set of berets in maroon or black. The boots are missing, but it doesn't matter. Africans get corns. They'd rather hunt rhinoceros barefoot. Them and the rhinoceros, barefoot."

"What are you going to do?"

"Sell them. Tomorrow I meet with Mokoena."

"Agamemnon Mokoena?"

"The same. Who gave him that name, do you know?"

"He's Greek, on his mother's side."

"He's black?"

"As the night. Color genes are dominant."

"Agamemnon...," he repeated, pensive. "Which one was he? The one from Mycenae?"

"For sure."

Next day, very early, he started downriver, dragging the trunk. I took up planting vegetables, which had been put off since our arrival. Theresa sank into deep reflection, sitting on her heels on a boulder or curled up under a bush.

Cerutti returned a week later, sweaty and disheveled, unshaven and a little leaner, still dragging the trunk.

"What a shit, man!" he burst out. His presence brought Theresa back from her long self-imposed ostracism. "I'd rather beg than try to do business with that guy again!"

While he prepared his *mate*, he briefly summarized his experience.

That guy, Mokoena, was insufferable. He felt one step away from victory, yet he wouldn't hear about buying uniforms. He had no intention of dressing his men as second-rate guerrillas. He idolized the Greek world and its Hellenistic legacy, as Cerutti quickly surmised. He was intent on creating an authentic democracy, like the original one, with all the people united in an assembly, perhaps using the Malabo stadium. He wanted to reproduce Attica, Athens and the Parthenon. Cerutti didn't see the problem. He was offering British uniforms, from the navy and army, two guarantors of one of the most solid parliamentary monarchies in the world, which today represented authentic Athenian ideals better than any other government. Why not dress in their shirts and insignias? The berets could be left aside, of course. It was a unique opportunity. Now or never. Otherwise, he would sell the whole lot to the Maoists of Sefatsa...

The deliberate mention of his rival managed to upset Mokoena, who forbade him to mention the name of the "traitor on Peking's payroll" in his presence ever again. Cerutti accepted the ban with some reservations. Mokoena reminded him that his was a triumphant revolution and he would soon enter Malabo victorious. So much the better, replied our friend. This was one more reason to buy the uniforms, since it was important to care for appearances upon entering the capital. Mokoena lost his temper again. Cerutti was very wrong again if he thought that Mokoena would be satisfied only with the capital. He meant to continue north, liberate the Sudan, penetrate into Egypt, reach the Mediterranean, and build a city bathed by its waters with a lighthouse and a library or an avenue of columns. Cerutti reminded him that Alexander had already done it and it had scarcely made a difference. Mokoena replied that until then nobody had ever dared critize his mother. Cerutti was baffled. Mokoena inquired calmly if he would rather be shot or fed his uniforms one by one, along with the trunk. Shooting would be quicker. Cerutti suggested that they might prefer to cook him in a big cauldron as done in old times. But at this point Mokoena, who was not gastronomically knowledgeable, had him booted out of his tent, trunk and all. "I have a revolution in progress," Mokoena shouted at him from the depths of his abode.

"Nicely put," I said. "And now what are you going to do?"

At the moment, the question about future plans seemed like a low blow, seeing him sitting on his trunk with one leg crossed at a sharp angle, dispirited, scratching his beard, a decent soul facing defeat.

"Sleep," he concluded resolutely.

And so he did. He slept for a whole week in a corner of the hut. Theresa and I stretched out by the fire that night and the next. On the third day she slipped out of my embrace and went to join Cerutti in the hut. She didn't come back.

5

I resolved to dig the well by the river, four hours in the morning and just as many in the afternoon, but the soil had hardened. I felt like a bird with its wings cut off, without ever having flown, not even once. Like one of those disheveled flamingoes or ostriches that occasionally wandered about the dried-up riverbed, not to quench their thirst anymore, but resigned to the solemnly awkward movement of their feet, the senseless haughtiness of their carriage, the deadweight of their disappointed hopes.

Having finished his rest period, Cerutti picked up his trunk and left again, while I was working inside the well. He was on his way to search for Sefatsa and his troops. (Theresa curled up under a bush again, self-absorbed and remote.) This time his absence was shorter. He returned in three days, still thinner, with the trunk on his shoulder.

"You sold a bunch," I guessed.

"The berets," he reported and Theresa clapped her hands like a child.

The ever underesti*mate*d Duma Sefatsa was something else. Cerutti couldn't understand why he was losing the war. It could be on account of the Chinese, who had never financed a guerrilla worthy of the name. For that very reason—the rather weak support—they needed to change their image, do something that would rekindle their well-deserved prestige as fighters: a set of berets, either maroon or black, for example, would do the trick. Sefatsa, smiling and fatherly, had listened to him while exchanging knowing glances with members of his joint command. Then he came up with a quotation from the Great Leader in reference to the rains falling on the Great Wall. Cerutti seemed to understand that he was on the right track and he opened up on the subject of the harsh weather on the damp pampas. Having been invited to dinner at the guerrillas' campsite, his brain saturated with apple brandy, he cheerfully accepted a promissory note to be paid in the capital in the presence of an officer of the embassy of the People's Republic of China. "This Sefatsa is something else," he concluded upon returning from the interview. "If I had the power, man, I'd take him into Malabo before Mokoena gets there so he could kick Mokoena in the ass until the crack disappears."

The next day he left for Malabo to cash in the promissory note. He returned at dusk, vomiting insults. The Great Leader, or rather his Peking successors, had systematically refused to open an embassy in Malabo. There had never been an embassy from the People's Republic of China in Malabo.

That evening by the fire, he methodically chewed up the promissory note and washed it down with a brisk swallow of Ballantine's, instantly reducing Duma Sefatsa to the same level as Mokoena in his personal configuration of hierarchies.

6

The last chance, the last possible buyer, was Rashola, Moses Rashola, the supreme power in Malabo, protected by his police force and a few regular soldiers who were about to desert.

"They already have uniforms," I warned him. "I think the English themselves provided them, some years ago."

"Yes, of course, many years ago. That's better, man. You know that with maneuvers and all, uniforms wear out."

"Are you going to do business with Rashola's government?" I inquired, appalled, starting a diatribe.

By nightfall the next day I'd censored his intentions with some heavy hints at the "warped ethics of those who do business in the trenches."

"They're like battlefield vultures," I declared, unable to get off the subject. "They fill their guts at the dead's expense."

He shrugged his shoulders.

"So what?" he retorted. "Vultures suffer from bad press, that's all. We do practically the same thing. Or do you eat the cow while it's still alive?"

He didn't even wait for an answer. Without the slightest sign of remorse, he sat by the fire and filled himself with *mate* until dark. Then he went into the hut to rest, and Theresa followed him. I stayed by the flickering fire and finished the Ballantine's, muttering pointless insults addressed to the "crime transnationals," the "dogs of war," the second-rate mercenaries and surreptitious invaders of humble African dwellings, who show up one day with trunks full of berets and epaulettes and little by little consume all your whisky, occupy your hammock and blankets and take over your hut without any authorization. They don't even think of suggesting that they might take a shovel to help dig the damned well that some international organization approved a long time ago, then filed among the less important documents, on the most insignificant chip of a misplaced computer stored on the highest floor of a building in Geneva or Brussels, where the blessed project and the well were described in great detail, away from the flies and starving ostriches who went on searching fruitlessly along the dry riverbed in Kangala, the country where an honorable man had to stay outside in the open, without due warning, forced to listen, between his ineffective insults, to an improvised couple shamelessly frolicking until dawn in the obliging darkness of the hut, his own hut, while the rhinoceros that occasionally showed up at night snorted among the tin cans in neighboring trash heaps.

It was the end. Time to leave the place and bid each other farewell before we could do each other harm. We only had a package of spaghetti and a can of tomatoes for the farewell dinner. Theresa brought some ominous looking mushrooms, thyme and caraway seeds and some other edible herbs. At noon the spaghetti was ready. Cerutti settled himself at the head of the table.

"As usual, man," he said, lifting his fork in his ritualistic gesture. "What matters most is to go on stirring things up."

He departed at nap time, dragging the trunk. At 7:00 I packed together the few things I had brought with me in my knapsack and started walking toward Malabo.

Only Theresa was left behind. From the nearest clearing I turned around for a last look at her, dazzling in her loincloth, one arm raised, with the savanna all around her, smiling by the well.

7

I never went home. Rashola's defeat, coinciding with Cerutti's death, caught me by surprise almost two years later (Mokoena and Duma Sefatsa took that long to unseat him). The news reached me through a dispatch from ORTF, in whose employ a cameraman and I were supposed to roam around Paris in search of intriguing news. We took no risks. We only had to avoid stepping on dog shit on the sidewalks.

In the next few months we got new reports originating from Kangala, but—as expected—no additional information about the Argentinean from the Malabo Palace after the cable mentioning the disappearance of his body from the morgue. The situation in Kangala was confusing. Sefatsa had entered the capital with Mokoena, thanks to a last-minute agreement, but the smell of luxury rugs and official dispatches had soon revived old rivalries between the two guerrilla leaders. Sefatsa threatened to return to the savanna while Mokoena thundered that he would push him all the way out there if he didn't go voluntarily. Under these circumstances, the ORTF assigned a team of correspondents to Kangala, and I signed on for the ride at the last minute.

Nothing seemed much different with Mokoena and his people in the government. At the airport, the tricolor standard of the Mokoena faction flew high with unjustified optimism next to the flag of Kangala. At the landing strip the potholes and cracks were the same as before. As we advanced toward the city, I felt deep melancholy. I had returned there to trace back the flow of memory, with the definite hope of finding Cerutti and his trunk again on some riverbank, but he was now buried deep in the ground (this was my only certainty as I moved toward Malabo), whereabouts unknown, and life was not an overflowing river running toward the sea in the natural process of dying, but scarcely a dried up, cracked bed of a nonexistent river that would never reach the ocean.

The next day, my ORTF colleagues spread out through the ministries to multiply the number of interviews with the revolutionary hierarchy, to guarantee the highest audience ratings among the metropolitan leftist elite. As for me, I disengaged early from the film team and caught a cab, a shabby relic from the former regime, and headed for the residential sector of the capital. I knew exactly where to go: the Argentinean consulate, which shared a floor with other diplomatic offices on the old Rashola Avenue, now called Liberation Avenue.

My ORTF credentials opened doors for me to see the consul. He was an affable individual with Arab features, long graying beard, large nose and lips, thick hair and big, crushing hands ready for uncontrollably strong handshakes. He looked like a Bedouin monarch finally rid of the camel culture, now exalted behind his desk, eager to make a good impression and cover up his sand and desert ancestry. Quite an Argentinean characteristic.

"You are from French television, aren't you?" he began, pointing to a chair. "Don't tell me, you are here to find out about a man called Cerutti."

So I didn't tell him. He was well-informed about the case in all its details, having conducted the investigation. A matter of human concern, he explained.

"Besides the lack of work, man, nothing happens here. I have never been so bored in my seventeen years as a consul. Because I started long ago, I want to make this clear from the beginning. Before the dead and all that... the disappearances, the 'sucking in' of people, who knows what else. I'm a career official. To me the dead all look the same, either red or yellow. It was my duty to investigate while the corpse was still at the morgue. You know that later it disappeared. Somebody took it away from the morgue. Perhaps they ate it, considering all the hungry rebels roaming around since then."

"Who killed him?" I asked.

"Nobody."

"How's that?"

"Frankly," he said, "the cause of death puzzled me as much as it does you. It seemed like something out of Agatha Christie. A guy with a bullet wound in his chest, found in a five-star hotel, spread over the bed, with several champagne bottles half empty on the nightstand, dressed in expensive clothes from Barney's, where only the English shop."

He hesitated a few seconds.

"It was simpler than I thought," he concluded. "The guy was selling uniforms. Nobody knows about that. Three days before Rashola's ouster, he sold a batch of British Navy shirts to the dictator's troops, after negotiating insistently for a year with the Minister of Finance. Almost all the troops deserted, taking the shirts with them, but Rashola paid cash so they would go well dressed. Thus he filled Cerutti's pockets at the last minute. This explains the luxury suite at the Malabo Palace. He went there to celebrate. A couple of days later Mokoena and Sefatsa enter the city with all their people on trucks, shooting their guns in the air. They had just driven by the hotel when the cleaning woman found Cerutti."

I sat stunned in my chair.

"Then..."

"One of those bullets shot into the air," my informant continued, "pierced a window of the Malabo Palace, just a small hole that nobody noticed at first. The bullet ricocheted off the ceiling and hit my countryman in the chest. This is one up on Agatha Christie, don't you think? Not even counting the disappearance of the body a few weeks later. Still, we must remember that this is not the first Argentinean who disappears without a trace these days. I can't imagine where he might be."

That afternoon I took a bus to the outskirts of town in search of an answer. Heading toward the past that was not to be the past. I had a certainty of this when I got off the bus and started walking toward the river. I expected to see the ramshackle hut built with wood planks and sheetmetal. It was there, but somebody had gone to the trouble of fixing it up, board by board. I expected to see emaciated ostriches and other birds in the desolate surroundings, but instead I saw chickens, a corral and vegetable garden. I expected to see a useless hole by the riverbed. The hole was there but the savanna had proceeded to fill it with water, the water had finally emerged from deep underground and someone with a persevering hand had turned it into a well. I expected to find a desert but there were more huts not far away, with gardens and corrals. I was prepared for absences, the implacable silence of the savanna; instead, Theresa's lined, yet still young face watched me with half concealed pleasure from the threshold of the hut. At her side, a small black boy of no more than two years of age picked freely at his nose, without taking his eyes off me. Not far from the hut I saw a wooden grave marker with flowers all around it.

That night we slept by the well, in each other's arms. The next day she went to a meeting in the neighborhood and I sat down for a while by the grave. Later I fetched a pail of water and sprinkled the flowers with it while the child watched my every move from near the hut. I deliberately poured some of the water on myself and he burst out laughing. It was Cerutti's laughter. Or mine? Theresa could not clarify this. It was the irrepressible laughter of a survivor within the heart of Africa, next to a grave, with a corpse close to our memories, not missing anymore but there, under the flowers, and a well overflowing near by.

A week later I resigned from ORTF by phone. I never went back.

The stay in Indochina had infected him with a fever for adventure, a certain addiction to epic happenings, although while there all he had to do was char the hide of some Asian guys from the air, usually at dawn, nothing particularly heroic. But after living twelve years in Saigon, nearing 50 years of age, the scent of napalm had become redundant, too familiar to his nose, and he requested his discharge from the Air Force, to which he was fully entitled. He returned to his town in Illinois as a retired colonel, and sat comfortably idle in his house in Arlington Heights, killing time watching TV in the afternoons. In the loneliness of those days, with no more skimming flights at dawn, he languished poignantly. He missed the children he never had; he missed his wife, who had died from a pulmonary complication a few days before his return from Saigon, thus refusing him a last kiss, the welcome that others enjoyed, taking with her all the questions the war in Southeast Asia left unanswered. There was no solution now. She was dead and the war was lost.

One day at the local supermarket—it would have been hard to imagine a better twist of fate—he found a biography of Columbus, Admiral of the Ocean, which he bought and devoured in less than a week and which, unexpectedly, left a deep impression. While in the Air Force he had learned to navigate small crafts. A couple of weeks after finding the book, after looking into the idea from a multitude of angles, he withdrew his savings from the bank and bought a frail, two-masted sailboat that he christened Guinevere in memory of his wife. In June of that year he dismantled the boat and sent it by air to Madrid. From there it went by train to Palos de la Frontera, where he purchased canned food and staples for three months, bottled water for six months, thirty liters of rum, a small petrol stove, Gershwin tapes, tobacco for his pipe and an inflatable boat as a precautionary measure. Before boarding he granted an interview to a radio station in Huelva interested in reporting to its listeners his desire to repeat Columbus' crossing of the ocean five hundred years later, an unusual yearning for a Vietnam veteran. The next day, on the dawn of the third of August, he finally set sail in the direction of the Canary Islands, the first port of call of the voyage.

He sailed at the will of the trade winds for almost two months. The "Rhapsody in Blue" comforted him in the solitude of the Atlantic Ocean, that and the rum he drank on deck from dawn to dusk, occasionally erring in his course, still under the spell of his high seas hero, with only a compass and quadrant to find his way, defenseless before the possible abyss, and with a flickering hope of seeing India or Cipango rise on the horizon.

In early October, as had happened five hundred years before, he saw a small island to the West. He assumed it must be one belonging to the Bahamas or Lucayas and proclaimed the discovery (Land!) to himself. When he was about a hundred meters from shore he noticed a cove and a line of small huts on the beach, thick smoke revealing the presence of humans, several canoes on the shining white sand and people squatting at the door of their dwellings. Fearing shoals and coral reefs, he dropped anchor and reached the shore in his inflatable boat, where the people greeted him with repeated and joyful slaps on the back. He remembered but then restrained himself from repeating the emotional words of Columbus in Guanahaní, the bartering of glass beads for manioc bread between the Admiral and his hosts. He gratefully accepted the bread, perhaps baked with manioc, and for a lack of necklaces and trinkets, he offered them the remains of his stock of rum. By sundown they were all drunk, chattering in a dialect made up of nasal sounds and shrieks, with toothless, candid jokes at the expense of the newcomer, his light colored eyes, his clothes (they all wore only loincloths), or his skin stark red from the sun (theirs being copper-colored). As night fell he sought shelter in a knotted hammock provided as an honor by the local chieftain, an affable, potbellied individual, covered with feathers and loads of necklaces. Through sign language the natives conveyed that there were no other inhabitants on the island, which they called Buri or Bungui.

In the night one of the daughters of the chieftain slipped into the hammock and explained, also by sign language, the basics of the local mythology. She mentioned a bearded sailor—he smiled, touching his unshaven face—who would arrive on the island to revitalize the land and its fruits by his presence, and that they must welcome and feed him. She herself took responsibility for the welcome, reactivating effortlessly his postponed virility, restoring to it the power that Southeast Asia and his wife had taken away. She wrapped herself around him in the hammock, rubbing against his body, gripping him with her lustrous haunches divided by the loincloth, making him feel young once more and on the prowl, eager with desire for that velvety dark rump, smelling of coral and sensuous adolescent fluids in her less accessible crevices. They ended up laying on the sand. She waited for him on her back, curling up when she felt him inside her, scratching his back without breaking his fair skin, kissing him wildly, pouring onto him the damp, free passion of her uncivilized lips, plunging her resolute tongue into his throat, then slowly sliding downward until finding the anxious appendage to his belly and taking the totem into her avid mouth, sucking it to suit her fancy, rubbing up and down with her lips, in a sweet, improvised token of cannibalism until forcing him to release himself in her mouth...no more than a second in the Caribbean night sheltered by that isle without a history and the soft murmur of the waves on the shore. She then abandoned him on the sand, exhausted, grateful, and indifferent to his boat and his past, detached beneath the stars.

After a week he decided to explore the place, going deeper into the vegetation up to the heights of the small island. There he was astonished to find an amphitheater carved in the rock. From that vantage point he scanned the horizon. In the morning silence he marveled at the reigning solitude and this unexpected discovery, a tribe of Caribbean natives still in the stage of loincloths and bare hanging breasts, oblivious to turbojets and toothpaste.

It was already early evening when he returned to the village. As he approached by the edge of the beach, he noticed an unusual number of fires and revelry and dancing by the sea. Somebody came to meet him and invited him to sit on a bamboo throne next to the chief, where they stuffed him for the hundredth time with their smoked meats and fermented drinks. Shortly after midnight he ended up listless in his hammock, incapable of ingesting anything more. The next morning the whole tribe woke him up and carried him on their shoulders to the forest, everyone smiling and chanting, the men wearing garish, wild masks, the women and children shaking gourd and cane rattles, dancing, writhing to the rhythm of the voices and choral refrains. He smiled reluctantly from a sense of obligation, wishing he could return right away to his hammock and forget for the rest of his day that outlandish crowd, bent on drinking and celebrating carnivals on any whimsical pretext. This time for just any bearded stranger arriving at their shores.

They didn't even give him time to be surprised. Nearby, just a few meters from their place in the heights he saw the amphitheater filled with smiling islanders. In the center he caught sight of the chieftain bedecked with his most precious feathers, holding in his right hand a sharp, shining object. He tried to protest, but someone stopped him, grabbing him violently from behind by the neck. From the back of the amphitheater a promising whiff of charred meat reached his nose, some animal roasting on the fire.

"Like in Indochina," he thought in awe, without any real desire to resist.

By no means would I alter, on account of obscure threats, my most deeply rooted habits, which included a brief evening stroll, stepping between the swastikas grossly daubed on the sidewalk under my feet. At most I avoided treading on them in order not to aggravate the perpetrators. There was no point in fueling their anger. At the beginning it seemed to me that the emblem was distributed haphazardly on the walls and narrow streets of the neighborhood, without a definite purpose, no direct intimation to me. But I soon realized that their locations were planned. They all led in a line to the door of the "old Professor." They clearly singled me out in a grotesque trajectory that invariably ended by our apartment on Bergasse, on the Danube's banks. Nevertheless, I refused to give up my strolls from our house to the river, following its banks for a while, then returning slowly, at a listless, indifferent pace. Haste is not a defense mechanism available to an octogenarian, not even for the privilege of being aware of surveillance in Vienna or now in London. With youthful vehemence, my daughter Anna opposed my senile wanderings in the neighborhood.

The swastikas and threats, the gold braid embroidered uniforms and the boots had left a scar in her spirit. Even today, far away from home, their harmful potential disturbs her and I understand why. She is young and a still fresh face is vulnerable to the boots and the damage they could inflict on it. That is not my case, nor was it in Vienna, when I roamed about the neighborhood at sundown, looking for a breath of fresh air near the Danube.

I had moreover other pastimes, my books, one or two remaining patients—among them Frau Skoff, Bertha Skoff, who became, thanks to her bold nature, the unexpected protagonist of my last days in Vienna. I would see her twice a week. She

reminded me, in her enveloping naturalness, of the case of Anna
O., a woman as voluptuous as she was exasperating, who
Breuer referred to my practice for reasons not completely clear,
possibly to test me. Vain strategy; I would not think of risking
my impeccable trajectory by eagerly flinging myself upon this
disturbing woman when she was so absorbed on the couch. For
months I had to fight off my erections, sitting in the chair behind
her. Something that I did not take down in my notes on Anna O.,
of course. Science must protect its customary disguises and
alibis.

In any case, age has weakened my will and professional
scruples, now that the theory has been established and nobody
expects great revelations in writing about *la chose sexuelle*.
Neither could I be shocked by Bertha's boldness when, during
our third session, she surprised me by staying silent for a long
while.

"What's happening?" I inquired.

"It isn't fair, doctor," she replied in a provocative tone of
voice.

"What isn't fair?"

"This way I can't talk to you sincerely. I need to look you
in the eyes."

A move calculated on her part to initiate from that flank the
desired profanation of the temple. From that moment on I
surmised that she would never again lie down on the couch, a
challenge that every competent analyst receives during his
career, an occupational hazard. At the next session I was able to
confirm it by looking at her sitting on the closest armchair, not
on the couch, scrutinizing me without compunction, a smile full
of suggestions on her ruddy face. I didn't even think of resisting.
Down deep I'm a romantic. Any of Schubert's works, even a
sonata, has more persuasive power over me than all of Descartes
and his impeccable reasoning. This suits a man advanced in age
suddenly confronting a young, well-built Austrian girl, with
curly hair and generous breasts. It was then that she talked to me
for the first time about her husband, whom she depicted as a
"repulsive bureaucrat," originally from Lower Austria, who
seemed impervious to some Viennese customs. To judge by her

description, he was extremely uncouth, primitive and ill-humored. He enjoyed pushing her around at night, like his riverside-dwelling ancestors did with the sheep and goats, to sodomize her at will. She participated in his habits at least at the rhetorical level. During our sessions she spoke about him as "the stallion" and "an insatiable stud." About the object between his legs, she described his attributes in a far more explicit manner. She characterized it either as "the salami" or "the sausage," and other such delicatessen products.

From the fifth session on, something changed in her mind and she was not satisfied by just looking at me from her armchair. Mind and action were synonyms to her, a single, delicious proof of irreverence. In a premeditated rapture of shamelessness—I know now that every one of her actions was premeditated—she observed me for a few seconds without uttering a word, then plunged with her resolute fingers toward my crotch, suddenly grabbing the "salami"—in this case my own—which, caught unaware, moved from its usual somnolence to the fierce condition of a reheated bratwurst. It is worth stating that the instrument is still excellently functional, perhaps because I have spent my life listening to the intimate obscenities of Christians and pagans. A way among many to exercise its erectile capacities.

Her cunning face was now scarcely centimeters from mine, her strawberry perfumed breath very close to my mouth. A young woman whose fingers delicately insisted in exploring between my legs.

"This way we won't get anywhere, Frau Skoff," I warned.

"Why not?" she answered defiantly.

No way to insist on rejection. A female hand wrapped around a male's instrument points directly to paradise and it's not easy to resist. Who would blame her and how could I force myself to find hypocritical reasons to refuse her? Or at that point to resist the splendor and renounce Sodom and Gomorrah without even a glance? She took it upon herself to eradicate this and any other doubts that might trouble me, determined, smiling constantly, watching me with her misty eyes like the Danube on a cloudy day. Oblivious to any scruples, useless scruples, she rummaged perfidiously, shamelessly in the area of my fly, opened it with both hands and seized its contents without hesitation, brushing it with her nails and warm fingers, rubbing it up and down. Quite against my best judgment I switched to a most indecorous position on the chair, both my arms hanging by the sides, my legs folded upward, curled up against the back of the chair like a contented, aloof feline by the fireplace.

"I have never seen one like this," she commented while reducing the pressure.

That got me back to my senses. She had stopped to scrutinize her prey that, for a minute, seemed to weaken, dispirited in her hands. She surely referred to some superfluous material that I was deprived of at an early age, like so many of Abraham's offspring. I found some comfort in the thought that a sincere penis, with no wrappings or maskings, should be more pleasant to the eyes in its deliberate helplessness.

That evening I walked with unusual disquiet along the river, indifferent to the swastikas on the sidewalk and their authors. Nevertheless, just a few meters from our door I noticed, for the first time, a trio of gray shirts standing guard in the area, watching their art work to protect it from the pounding of my heels, as though somebody had warned them about my itinerary.

On Saturday I brought up the subject with the Princess, my aristocratic protectress in those days, a purebred Buonaparte who by reason of lineage was reticent about mass parades, no matter what the affiliation or emblems might be. She used to visit me once a week to dwell on the surrounding dangers and the need to leave the country. This time I saw her furrow her brow, perhaps as a sign of disbelief. It is well known that my ancestry nurtures an inveterate paranoia. She later suggested the possibility of contacting the Americans about the passports once and for all.

"It will be the same as in Berlin, Professor," she said sadly. "And in Germany the wisest have left a long time ago."

But I could not resign myself to the possibility of fleeing. During the eighth session, Bertha finally decided to approach me with her lips. It was the oral phase, which burst into fullness that day, after she had talked to me at length about her husband. Shortly before ending the session she sighed sorrowfully, stretched her hand toward my belly, brought out from its dwelling the little animal and fell on her knees. After that the deluge, in quite a literal sense. First, an imperceptible play of her prodigious tongue on the instrument, followed by a voracious rapture that led to a total absorption between the corners of her mouth, sucking it urgently in her burning, overwhelming jaws. It was a return to origins, a renewal of the fundamental pact, the rib and the mud, the serpent and the apple, with Lucifer lurking in the branches, Eve kneeling by the couch and Adam (yours truly) about to slide off the chair again.

"I have never seen one of these," she reiterated with a shaky voice, a by now well-known fact.

"You refer to the absence of some accessories?" I asked, but there was no answer. She had once again filled her mouth and couldn't speak...swallowing with delicious aggressiveness whatever she could get...squeezing it between her lips...stroking with her delicate shameless fingers the joyful epidermis of my genitals...a bold and insistent caress...the exact amount of friction to increase passion and leave me limp as a rag on the armchair while with feminine talent and the rhythmic movement of her lips she would bring forth the desired release...the decisive flooding to fill her mouth with promises...rejecting my weak protests or any sign of guilt with a sweeping gesture...compensating me for a whole life of frustrating postponements, sitting by the couch...waiting for her thirsty lips.

That evening I ecstatically, joyfully went astray once more by the Danube, like an adolescent after his first amorous rendezvous. For the first time in many years, I forgot my mouth ailment, and I even surreptitiously lit a cigar, oblivious to the ghostly and persistent images of my guardians, keeping my back turned to their gray uniforms.

Several days later they decided to launch an offensive. The local chief of police sent us an official notice that my distressed daughter was the first to read. If I insisted on my daily strolls in the neigborhood I would have to stick the Star of David on my lapel. Anna perceived not only a warning in this message, but an insult, no doubt about it. I didn't think so. David is the source of all that is ours; with him everything worked fabulously well for our people. Why would I feel ashamed to wear his emblem on my lapel? The swastikas would be spread under my feet on the sidewalk. Judea's emblem would blaze incorruptibly on my breast.

That night I cut the six-pointed star from a piece of cloth while Anna reproached me, standing by the window, watching the outside. Another visit from the Princess the next morning dissuaded me from attaching the star to my clothes.

"They will beat you up," she said persuasively. "And neither you nor I can take that at our age."

I opted for retiring to my office with my notes about Moses, which I have expanded here in London, notwithstanding my scant liking for the man. All he does is forbid and threaten, like my most recent persecutors. His problem certainly originated in a genital conflict. I imagine him angry and alone on the heights of Canaan, while his people yielded to boisterous frolic around the golden calf that everyone preferred. Something quite understandable amidst the desolation of the desert and its sands, where a calf may be an ideal complement to the crotch.

Then the old man returned from the mountains telling the story about his talk with Yahweh and his appalling Ten Commandments. A cunning way to channel his most intimate and senile twitchings! Old age, no doubt, provokes rhetoric.

It has happened, indeed, to many of my colleagues and adversaries, all of them one step from the old folk's home. I'd rather not talk about them; history will certainly acknowledge their achievements and omissions. Only Nietzsche, that irascible, nasty character, probably deserves a footnote, taking into consideration Goebbels and company's enthusiasm about his writings. I met him at the turn of the century thanks to Lou Andreas Salome, who was involved with him. Salome—I like to address her by her last name which recalls a certain biblical homicide of importance—insisted that we all three meet at her place. At the time I was more interested than necessary in cocaine and its deceitful properties. I suggested that we snort a bit to break the ice. It was not a good idea; we had barely tasted it when the guy started to howl something about the Antichrist and Salome chose to take off her blouse and corset, two of her favorite pastimes. We all three ended up in the ample bed of my friend, euphoric, bent on investigating a tripartite action between the sheets. In view of her experience in the matter, Salome assigned the positions. She knew how to give each one his due and what was best for all, without making subtle discriminations. That time she proceeded to taste successively the instruments. Then she used her skillful hands to lightly touch our most private interstices, alternatively or simultaneously, with exacerbating feathery caresses until we found ourselves, all three, kneeling on the mattress, she in the middle, her mouth clinging to my rival's rather considerable accessory. I placed myself in back of her, keenly aware of the rhythm of her shiny rump, wanting to explore with my lips the aromatic gap between her buttocks and fill my mouth with her perfume, then succumb with my penis between her thighs... in feverish swinging on the bed, all three soaked in sweat...an insolvable tangle of hands and feet, and the shared swaying in that room now impregnated with atavistic bodily essences while our friend made some extemporaneous references to the Antichrist. Salome shrieked and I enumerated select obscenities in her ear to flatter her, all in a three-voiced frenzy and a final uncontrolled uproar of curses, supplications and pantings on top of the mattress.

We were so young!

Sadly, dawn managed to dissolve the magic spell. I woke up startled with Salome by my side. Nietzsche was already dressed and he stared at us from his chair with a threatening expression on his face. Without even saying good-morning, he uttered stentoriously some hint at the "Sons of Abraham," who according to him lacked "the most elementary carnal attributes necessary to please a lady." Having said this, he grabbed his hat and left. This provided a favorable juncture to demonstrate the opposite to Salome, amidst renewed moans and yells from both of us at breakfast time.

From that day on, my good friend started to visit me assiduously at my office. "To complete your apprenticeship," she explained to me one day at the Cafe Sacher. After this the frustrated lover rushed forth in vitriolic writings against Christianity. I don't believe it necessary to remind anybody that the famous Jesus Christ was a misguided member of my tribe, not his.

An insatiable spirit, beautiful Salome. For her, oysters and white wine, as well as a certain preference for rear guard attacks, "per angostam viam," that revealed in her an anal fixation which almost cost me a divorce. On the other hand, easy going Mahler found the inspiration for his fifth symphony in her. Or was it the fourth?

A memorable epoch, no doubt. Together we shaped the dazzling Viennese turn of the century, of which only the spoils remain. All united in body and soul, if only by our common addiction to Salome's fickle rump.

As it began to happen to me with Bertha's. Anyhow, her insistence on suction worried me. In the latter phases of the clinical process I eagerly expected to lead her toward other possibilities, first, the back door (would it compare to Salome's?) and then to the regular channel until satisfactory completion of her libidinal evolution. All this providing that the club-wielding fanatics allowed us enough time.

We were getting close to the nineteenth session when the American ambassador, yielding to the Princess's pressures, came to personally give us our passports and visas at our apartment on Bergasse. One of his aristocratic friends who was then working at the Propaganda Ministry had warned him that the SS were ready to strike our neighborhood at any moment. Apparently somebody had informed them about my clinical practice and my schedule, and they'd already assigned me to a comfortable barracks somewhere far away.

"They have been waiting for you in London for months, Professor. You will have to leave the country this week, there is no alternative," the ambassador advised.

It was quite true: there was no other option. At least Anna took him at his word. At noon she started packing my belongings, books, letters, the Egyptian icons, Moses manuscript and other goods in order to ship them to London the next day. I refused to dismantle my office, in spite of the eagerness with which the British were prowling around my couch.

"They want it for a museum in your honor," the American ambassador whispered to me, as if speaking to a child.

This increased my anxiety. I didn't feel in the mood yet to get along, under the same roof, with the mummified exhibits at the Louvre or the British Museum, but time was getting short.

On Tuesday the Princess made reservations for us for a compartment on the Paris Express due to leave Friday night. That same day I called Bertha and scheduled her for Thursday, telling her that I was leaving for England. This would be our last session. On the telephone, she seemed less surprised than I expected.

Wednesday evening I took a last stroll through Vienna, my soul drenched with imminent nostalgia. Every stretch of the neighborhood, the riverbanks, the bridges spanning the flowing waters, the decrepit eagles spread over the imperial buildings, the tramways running toward the Schönbrunn palace, everything brought back some previous incident. My whole life was linked to those places, everything still within reach of my shaking hand to enjoy for the last time, indifferent to the stridence of the most recent banners, already resigned to oblivion in other latitudes, probably in the clamorous vicinity of Picadilly Circus. And never again to see the swans. Never again the clandestine, irreproachable excitement of lovers in the vicinity of Karlskirche. Never again the penumbra of the Volksoper, or Bertha, her orange tinted curls between my legs.

Unaware, I walked all the way to the Hofburg and from there, by small alleys, to the Stadtpark gardens where the municipal orchestra played Strauss waltzes in the open air. Nothing could be more appropriate for the occasion. I stopped by the grove of trees, behind the tables, to observe one or two couples who danced to the sound of "Southern Roses." It looked like an old print, a moment stolen from a calendar, when there was peace. Ruddy, arrogant individuals watched the scene from the tables. Among the trees, I avidly savored the moment.

In spite of the gold braid, the uniforms, the boots, the waltz would survive, impervious to events, ready for the day when the best of the Viennese spirit would revive.

It was then, at the last chords of "Southern Roses," that I saw her. Rather I recognized her among the other couples, being led through the waltz with martial steps by a man in uniform. A curly haired woman and a minuscule metal skull among her companion's golden braids. It was Bertha, led in the waltz by an SS officer. And she looked ecstatic!

I remained among the trees, overwhelmed, at a loss about what to do. Seconds later the orchestra gave way to the "Blue Danube." The two left the open air dance floor arm-in-arm and proceeded toward the gravel path. They stopped a few steps from the place where I was hiding. He grabbed her with his pale, cadaverous hands and whispered in her ear some obscenity that made her laugh. Then he uttered a compelling proposition.

"There, behind the monument to Strauss!"

They walked together toward the spot (and I followed furtively) where they fell into a violent embrace, hurriedly shedding their clothing. He kept the boots and the cap on, the metal skull prominently displayed. She wore only her stockings and corset. To the beat of the distant, disturbing rhythm of the waltz, both standing and almost naked, they voraciously, compulsively, violently went over each other with their lips until they dropped on the grass, rolling, biting, sucking each other in turn, she kneeling between his hairless legs, he with his hands clamped on her breasts pulling them brutally out of her corset to squeeze them while grunting mindless compliments. "Good work, little one, you were great…" Against the bloodied backdrop of the sunset, I glimpsed his insolent mouth, the glinting teeth ready for laughter or fury, it made no difference to him. I stood petrified among the trees, a persistent and pained voyeur who now listened to both lovers panting in the dark, with Strauss presiding undaunted on his pedestal and Bertha finally out of control, intent now on well-known gastronomic endeavors while her partner ordered her to turn around, to stay crouched on hands and knees on the grass, rubbing her breasts against the wildflowers of the municipal park, to demand her due from her uniformed partner (perhaps the same who sent her to my office?), urging him hoarsely to perform his part in the agreement. "Stick it in, now!" Eve once more surrendering to the serpent, this time the martial fallen angel that now invaded her buttocks from the rear, ready to take the sacrifice and his triumph, with the victim firmly in his claws, giving way to the last rattles and moans, while the waltz rose in the background with loud laughter in the distance, perhaps sinister Lucifer lurking in the branches, always watchful over his emissaries' pleasures.

And Bertha crouched in the mud, delightedly submissive to the passion that impaled her from behind, an instant of pleasure and pain, pleasure again, a final rattle and then the void, the fall, everyone expelled from paradise, the masters of power and their spies all into the pit, as it was already happening in Dachau, in Treblinka, Bergen-Belsen, one sole, extraordinary fire spread all over the earth...

Shaking, I returned to my apartment on Bergasse. That night I stripped the office, gathered my diplomas and photographs. I didn't need them anymore. As expected, Bertha Skoff didn't return to my office the next day for our final session. She had just completed, in her own way, the therapeutic process. Perhaps nothing remained to be done but the report to her superiors: the old man is leaving. Case closed.

round trip ticket

I think of you, Maria Helena, when walking down to the platform and boarding the night train to Barcelona, the nine-thirty express where I now skim through the newspaper bought as I passed through the Chamartin station. The compartment begins to fill up with voices and anonymous faces, greetings mechanically repeated and spontaneous agreements on the assignment of spaces. Mine is number eighteen, but it's the same to me if you prefer to sit by the window. While I circumspectly review the newspaper, carefully reading the summary of yesterday's events, I remember—I don't know why, but all memories of love seem to obey inscrutable laws—a distant evening in Madrid when we read in the press, laughing our heads off, that a man was to attend the funeral for his leg, which had been amputated a week earlier. Someone from the clinic gave it to him wrapped in polyethylene, for reasons not quite clear—something to do with urban pollution—so that he could get rid of it himself. At present this seems less funny to me, really it was definitely macabre. But at the time everything was just pure, irrepressible joy to us, and the ephemeral tragedies of others were no more than an occasional, brief report in the paper's section of unusual events. At the time we could laugh readily about the black humor of a Spanish citizen whose loss of his right leg allowed him a first contact with the cemetery, inevitable destination for practically everybody. We boasted of a renewed and superficial existentialism that had surprised us both in the golden, evasive happiness of our voluntary exile in a capital of old Europe. We had left behind forever (that's what we thought then, when we didn't yet participate in the compulsive search for news about the crisis in Central America or other harassed places in the continent, refusing to add our own nostalgia to that of other émigrés) the dictators and persecutions, the cemetery that several generals had created in our longed for (in spite of everything) fragment of the universe. Life, such a pompous word, was a mimicry of uncertainty, the most comfortable uncertainty. We read Unamuno and Valle Inclán, grateful to the Spain that greeted us with open hands and a peaceful heart. We were young, Maria Helena, and in love. At the scarcely attended bar of the Air France Jumbo we exchanged our first toasts, to eliminate any likely coincidence, convinced that our paths had already become superimposed, in this moment, over the Atlantic, while on our cheeks the taste of farewells still lingered, the sweet reminiscences of our native land.

The train starts slowly on its journey, the first tenuous jolts dispel my drowsiness, my body feels awkward and light on this departure. Chamartín moves backwards while my mind also recedes to the past and the first days in Madrid, when everything for us was a yearned-for dazzlement and shared roaming along the Gran Vía, during that unexpectedly cordial encounter with our ancestry. The motherland was recently delivered from its chains, from crosses and swords, a Spain we already knew from hearsay in the passionate memories of a distant relative, some errant republican who had preceded us in a reverse exile. From our room in a downtown hotel we leapt, irreproachably, victoriously, to the sidewalks to lose ourselves in a cinema or a concert—so much to see, so much to catch up on—to laugh together in an embrace in front of a shop window or try grimaces addressed to no one, a whole set of gestures that gradually identified us, and bound us together. Then we felt no nostalgia, nor were we aware of what a friend, steeped in sad wine, would later suggest to us in a bar at the Plaza Mayor: that even voluntary exile means discovering new roads at every turn, yet always wearing the same shoes impregnated with the dust of the distant homeland. The same old, worn-out shoes.

I think about all this while the train leaves Chamartín with exceptional punctuality, and abandons the passing landscape on the other side of the window on which I now lean my face. The universe of the capital at dusk will slowly be covered by shadows under the still lavender sky, all possible shades of red mixed into the last clouds, the always indescribable agony of sunsets on the Castilian plains. Something starts to throb uncontrollably inside me, something rises without warning to my eyes, forcing me to pick up the newspaper again, losing myself in blurred headlines that I can't understand, that I can't read anymore. Barcelona and you await me in the distance, that's all. I know now in the restricted ritual of a night train bound for the Mediterranean and Barcelona-Sants, the terminal station, amidst that fleeting, arbitrary linkage of the journey's participants. People who yesterday didn't know each other and now must necessarily get along until the end of the journey, obeying the improvised order that the ticket sales have determined in a coach lit only until eleven or a few minutes past, when the time comes to open the berths and every transitory occupant of the compartment yields to the scarcely restorative sleep in night trains.

A young man, no more than twenty years old, has brought a radio with him from which emerges with some difficulty an old Aznavour song: "Venice without You." Exactly this, Maria Helena, it can't be just a coincidence; not this, not here, precisely today. Outside it's already dark, suddenly night, and the lights of the urban periphery race to the capital, pulled along by the electric network. Darkness will soon envelop us, the real darkness outside the train, and Aznavour, "the deep emotion of remembering yesterdays" these people who travel with me to Barcelona, these good people who know nothing about me and still less about you, will become my only and most definite comfort, the only light amidst so much night.

"I'm in the service," I hear the young man say while he desperately tries to rescue Aznavour from the static.

There is no need for further provocation. His remark sparks a shallow, irrelevant dialogue. A man who looks like a banker is of the opinion that the "mili" isn't that bad after all. The young man disagrees. In no time at all we shall be no more than a memory of the night before, a sudden flash in the retina, each one back to his own affairs and occupations. The kid to finish his military service, an older man to the ceremonious gestures appropriate to retirement, a woman to her husband's arms awaiting her at the terminal. And myself to you, Maria Helena, for a much needed last minute reckoning.

The older man complains that he can't sleep a wink on trains, in spite of modern comforts, notwithstanding the berth and his frequent journeys between Madrid and Barcelona, working as an insurance agent until scarcely three years ago, obliged to travel all over the peninsula, well paid but a hard job.

We are getting close to Arcos de Jalón, they tell me, where the train stops for a few minutes. The dialogue continues without purpose. In the background I hear the radio broadcaster explaining Aznavour's decline in the hit record ratings, something inevitable—in his opinion—within the ethereal universe of music's fashions. "We are nothing," he ends philosophically, referring to our most probable course, the meaningless void we shall all leave behind when we depart.

I feel I have no right to such considerations, my sweet comrade, you know this better than I do, better than the guy on the radio. You told me so, vehemently, in Madrid when our relationship—why?—went to the dogs. Yet it doesn't matter much now. Against the implacable background of memory, my agonized reminiscing, all that is left is this compartment of the National Railroad Network, where my hopes falter at the rhythmic pace of the coach and yield to an absurd, forgettable dialogue that performs the miracle of distancing me now and then from nostalgia. And I think it isn't too bad just to be an undefined number amidst these people, one more passenger, never again a foreigner, never again who I was until yesterday, until the precise instant when I received the cable sent from Barcelona; never again the fainthearted individual who occasionally held you in his arms or enjoyed the right to immerse himself with you in the bookshops near the university. And I'm not sure why I'm going now to find you in Barcelona. Will it be possible to renew everything once more, even for a few hours? Something—either a flash of modesty or fear—tells me, in spite of all, that it might be better to stay here indefinitely, in the interregnum of this train coach, without time or past. Clinging to the profile and demeanor of a conventional citizen, stuck with the rest of the passengers. I shall relinquish my round trip ticket to Barcelona to the inspector (what he calls the "billete," instead of "boleto") for him to perforate, restoring my right to stay a few more hours in this no man's land. Nobody will know my name, nobody will remember my features nor ask questions about us: nobody knows that yesterday I read that cable a thousand times to convince myself that the name appearing in it was yours. The conversation continues past midnight in the compartment, it pleasantly feeds on itself; nobody wants to sleep yet. I turn once more to the limp newspaper on my lap. I haven't even gone beyond the international news. In some fold of the pages assigned to the provinces, there must be additional data, written as fast as the teletypes go, waiting to grab me by the throat and offer me a compendium of names and details, information I don't need. The kid places his radio in the luggage rack, initiating with this gesture the night's activities. Everyone stands up, blankets and pillows are distributed. It's time to sleep.

Time to go out on the corridor to find some fresh air and a smoke.

Outside the compartment, against the backdrop of the night landscape in the window, I meet a young man, fatigue showing on his face, leaning on his own thoughts. He can't sleep either. He offers me a cigarette and we introduce ourselves. He is deeply interested in South America, that must be like a fresh version of Spain, he tells me. He would like to visit my country some day. For a second I'm tempted to speak to him about you, about us, but I restrain myself. It's better this way. Tobacco smoke weaves between us an inconsequential dialogue that is all I need right now to finally disengage myself from the past, to obliterate from my mind your smiling image on the Gran Vía and reject the compulsive inventory of always insufficient reasons that led us to part. At this hour of night—it's already dawn—the past fades, wrapping itself up, like Madrid, in a dark distance, impossible to encompass. All I have left now is the rhythmic clattering of the train. Now we're passing Zaragoza; Barcelona is just a few hours away, which doesn't make it any closer, Maria Helena. In spite of the clock and stations in between, it will continue to be for me a city I didn't discover with you, it will have no shared memories, the chairs and walls of an urban cafeteria will never bring back your image. In spite of myself, you have remained in a corner of old Madrid, in the platforms of Chamartín where almost a year ago I went for our good-byes and we kissed with deceptive formality, avoiding tears with great propriety, expressing the certainty of an imminent reunion although we both knew that was a beautiful, necessary falsehood. There wouldn't be—most probably—another chance for us. Barcelona, summarized in a friendly postcard, had fascinated you, it was possible to be perfectly happy on the avenue by the sea at sundown, everything pointed to a necessary renewal and "I love you always, very much, my comrade of the Gran Vía." After a short while I found part of myself in other arms, and never even felt the need to respond to a greeting that at the time seemed expendable to me.

Now I know that it was not expendable. That I too should have left the turns of the Gran Vía to find you again in Barcelona, far sooner than this day that begins gradually to grow, imperceptibly, on the long windows of the train. My improvised companion in the corridor interrupted the conversation around five o'clock: he might be able to catch some sleep before arrival. We are already close to our destination.

He is right. About two hours later the train finally enters the urban periphery of Barcelona and at 7:40 we slide circumspectly, with a last gentle move from the engineer, into Barcelona-Sants station. The wheels squeaking on the tracks, a warning blast of the whistle to the people on the platforms, a last tired bellow announces the end of the journey. It's time to jump to the platform. Time to give a hurried good-day, return blankets and pillows where they belong, rub our eyes and comb our hair. The retired gentleman refutes himself and announces that he slept splendidly and now, gentlemen, here we are, it's been a pleasure, the city waits for all those who now congregate anxiously at both ends of the car waiting for their turn to descend the stepladders.

It's Barcelona, Maria Helena, here I am, finally. But something prevents me from joining the flow of the other passengers. Something tells me that it's too late, that as usual it's hopeless.

I can't leave the train. All I have left is the sleepy space of the now empty compartment, where I remain entranced, watching the embraces and back slapping of the relatives on the platform, the smiles of those who arrive and those waiting for them. And I long to smile also, to continue to be part of them. But it's too late, they begin to leave, walking down the platform, and I'm still in the car, on the other side of the window, anchored to my memories. I can't leave the car now, to enter the city you came to a little over a year ago. Somewhere in it, far away from our country, your body lies carrying the imprints of the accident. Your face is intact, but your heart is still, forever still. The consulate will take care of documents and transportation, the dry announcement to your family: an automobile accident on the highway to Gerona. You will return finally, my love, wearing the same old shoes, but before long, before all this, I will have abandoned you once more. Because I will not go now to catch the metro. I will stay in this car waiting for its return to Madrid. In the capital I shall find again your image unharmed. In Madrid you will still be standing and I will be able to roam arm in arm with you against the forgotten backdrop of a glass of beer at the Záhara or at the tables set on the flagstones of the Plaza Mayor. And I shall continue to leaf through the newspaper looking for the strange events section, smiling at the reports about people who attend the funeral for their own leg, those who on the threshold of death can still joke and laugh openly. That's enough for the time being. Don't ask me to go and look at your coffin in the midst of a city that doesn't belong to us. Forgive me, Maria Helena, for this grandiloquent evasion, for this my final weakness.

By the enormous Lake of Geneva, with his bodyguards at his heels, Leontiev evoked the beginning of his career in Stalingrad during the Teutonic army's siege, around '42. Among the debris, hunger and the dead, he had engaged in the first games against some partisan separated from his battalion, eager—as he was—for a respite at the chessboard, in the irrelevant domain of bishops, castles and knights. His opponent at the time was not a poor chess player, perhaps somewhat scattered in his strategy with a tendency to advance all his pieces in the first moves, moving his pawns, knights and bishops forward until filling the center of the chessboard, most probably a legacy of his partisan activity; the frontal, reckless attack and the irrepressible desire to define the situation in the very first moves. Leontiev himself considered each move at length before proceeding; this came to exasperate his opponent who would taunt him with sarcastic remarks while waiting for his turn. Flustered, Leontiev would get a hold of any minor piece, a pawn or knight, moving it to a safe, non-threatened position. That is how he managed to defeat the partisan the first time.

"Checkmate," he now thought by the formidable Geneva ocean, and he crossed the Pont des Bergues to reach the square honoring Rousseau, "citoyen de Genève," as explained by the monolith on which he rested his elbows, smiling. The bodyguards remained on the bridge, keeping a prudent distance. Under cover of the shadows, the champion enjoyed again his baffling triumph over the partisan (how long ago!), by moving forth, from the rear, the less important pieces. Later, among the ruins of Stalingrad, on a rusty dusk twilight, it took him several hours to discover the clue, the secret of his unexpected victory. Infuriated, the partisan demanded another game, an immediate retaliation, yielding the white pieces with reluctant benevolence, the privilege of opening the game. Leontiev retreated behind a line of pawns again, refusing the unpremeditated attack against enemy territory. And he won again, the next match and all that followed as well. The next day his competitor claimed the pretext of having to rejoin his battalion. Intrigued, Leontiev returned to his home where he tried to reproduce some of the games. There absolutely had to be a common denominator, something that would explain the victorious turn of events on the chessboard.

At some unknown hour of dawn he left his bed, and with the help of a candle proceeded to scrutinize the cheap editions lining the shelves in his room. Among them in a prominent place he found *The Communist Manifesto*, the volume printed in Kiev that his father had given him as a present before leaving for the south to participate in the final encounter with the hooves of the "whites" that ravaged his face. He lingered on its pages ("…a phantom roams in Europe…") until morning broke loose in the window, a new daybreak with birds and omens of collective redemption. Amid their initial hesitant warbles, later impetuous, Leontiev finally realized: the pawns, they held the key. The least flamboyant section of his army, the lowliest, simple contingent, opening fire in any game and keeping the enemy at a distance. A queen could encompass the chessboard at will. The bishops and the castles likewise…on condition that there were no rival pawns on the lurk. Whoever tries to control everything could be exposed to lose it all and himself at any moment. The loss of the queen was irreparable, the death of a pawn was usually irrelevant, and that was its strength.

The local representative of the Chess Society, linked to the Soviets, freed him of the sentence that doomed him to linger forever on the provincial postwar chessboards, by reporting his talent to the Party's leadership. At twenty-five he was summoned to Moscow to compete in the first national tournament with five contestants from each republic. He demolished Ukrainians and Russians, some Mongols, and two Lithuanians. In less than a month he was proclaimed the undisputed leader of the tournament, which entitled him to kisses on the cheek from

Beria, and even from the Iron Man himself. Later he described the details of his strategy in writing. It consisted wholly on turning, from the beginning, to pawns and other lesser pieces, aligning them at the back of the chessboard and then catching the rival unaware, by the rearguard, at the moment called "Leontiev's defense," which prompted favorable comments from *Pravda*. "Comrade Leontiev," wrote an editor at the time, "summarizes the best qualities of our system in his chessboard strategy: the unlimited reliance on the ideals of justice and solidarity. The world must be told that all traces of monarchy and feudalism are doomed to disappear under the irresistible advance of its former vassals and peons, the anonymous and fraternal army that strikes from the back, from the slums of history and the chessboard, to define the final checkmate on the enemy king and his preceding masters."

"Good times," thought the champion, while night descended over the lake and the undaunted waters of the Rhône. Some anonymous official at the Geneva city hall had just touched the switch that turned on the lights along the waterfront and by the gigantic fountain close to the square. At that moment something, someone, drew his attention toward the entrance to the bridge. A tall and ungainly individual was crossing with light and fast steps on his way to the Hotel D'Angleterre, where the Federation had assigned lodgings to the Soviet player, his retinue, and to the African, his opponent, the latest candidate to the crown. He recognized him by his skin and a fleeting flash of his teeth in that face as black as the night. He remembered a photograph published by the *Frankfurter Allgemeine* the day before. Anibal Kane, Mauritanian, unknown until a couple of years ago, who in one stroke had eliminated the great international masters in the preliminary phase. From his village in the African bush he had arrived to increase the ranks of the anointed, until winning his right to Geneva and the luxurious hotel suite toward which he now walked with a light step. From his vantage point in the square, Leontiev saw him cross the Pont des Bergues—his own bodyguards had turned to watch him, momentarily neglecting the champion—and he smiled indulgently to himself. Nothing better than that youngster, a bastion of ever disregarded Africa, to crown his effort and career. He might be a remote descendant of the brave Masai (his considerable height pointed in that direction). Through the media reports, the Soviet's champion was aware of his eccentric behavior at earlier tournaments. Might he have read in his straw hut, under the searing sun of northwestern Africa, the textbook written by Leontiev himself? It was quite possible that some French publisher had issued it a few years earlier; the distance between Paris and Mauritania is not forbidding. The next day, during the inaugural game, he would find out. For the time being, he watched him disappear alone in the dusk's gathering shadows, without a retinue or the unavoidable prestige of a world crown on his head.

***

The encounter was scheduled at four o'clock in the hotel's "Hunter's Hall." The initial drawing of lots had favored Leontiev. It was his turn to open the games. At the door he dismissed his bodyguards, smiled to the television cameras and strode toward his place by the chessboard. To his amazement, which was shared by the select audience assembled by the stage, Kane had not arrived yet. Nothing extraordinary; Mauritania is not London, no one originally from that region had reason to practice punctuality, except those involved with Nigerian Television, which had been the first to arrive to cover the event and broadcast its particulars to most of the few African viewers interested in chess. "Tarzan and his family included," the Italian commissioner of the Federation had said the day before, which caused a reprimand to be issued by his colleagues. At 4:03 everyone was excitedly aware of Anibal Kane's arrival at Hunter's Hall, dressed—it had happened in previous confrontations—according to his country's usual etiquette, in a light blue tunic, felt sandals and bracelets on both arms.

"No lion skins," thought Leontiev with relief. "After all, it's not so bad." Two members of Kane's delegation escorted him to the chessboard. Upon stepping on the stage, one of them turned to the audience and pronounced two words, no less amazing because they were few.

"Stand up!"

Nobody moved. Leontiev, who at that point happened to be standing up, looked at the Federation's president for a moment, smiled, and with a gesture invited the audience to rise. The confident expression on his face seemed to suggest "African eccentricities." Once this requirement was satisfied, Kane's spokesman stepped forward.

"His Serene Highness, Anibal Kane," he announced in French, "just crowned Prince of Kane, by the will of Allah."

Kane remained impassive. Then he turned to Leontiev, greeted him in the Muslim manner and took his place by the chessboard, much to the relief of the audience as well as the President of the Federation.

At 4:05—a five-minute delay that the champion courteously failed to claim on his behalf—Nikolai Leontiev started the game with the king's pawn to teach the Mauritanian youngster some humility and the sacred value of formalities.

***

"What happened, Nikolai?" inquired Shukov from his armchair.

It was impossible to answer that question at such an early morning hour under the bitter undertow of awakening with the sting of defeat inside him, a most unexpected and ragged defeat at the hands of Anibal Kane, Prince of Kane, by the will of Allah.

"I don't know," replied the champion in a frail voice, his face half hidden under the blankets. On the night table the breakfast tray remained untouched.

Shukov had just walked into his room unannounced and was sitting in the armchair closest to him, asking questions while indifferently examining his fingernails.

"It's not possible, Nikolai," he remarked with deliberate mildness. "There has to be a reason."

"Right now I don't know what it is, Marshall."

"What do we do now?"

"What concerns me right now is to have my breakfast. Afterward I shall study the match with Heifetz."

"When?"

"Today. This is just beginning, we have more than enough time. Relax, Shukov. He is just a lucky black."

There were not many blacks with good luck, at least not in Africa, except perhaps among the tribe's bureaucrats. Or some improvised monarch just crowned among the clamor of mud, mosquitoes and leprosy. Like this Kane character, emerged from nowhere and with no lasting tradition, come to humiliate him without warning at the first match for the title.

Shukov, sitting on the armchair, continued with his disquieting manicure.

"Do you want something else?" inquired Leontiev, examining the contents of the breakfast tray.

"A reason, Nikolai. Something to tell the Secretary."

"These things happen, Shukov. Stop fucking with me. Up to a certain point chess is unpredictable. Once I have analyzed the game with the others, I will have an answer. Now, if you don't mind, I want to be alone."

The Marshall looked at him with a stern expression, then rose from the armchair. He walked toward the door, and Leontiev thought he seemed older and more stooped than on other occasions, lacking his former impressive bearing. He was a haughty general of the Red Army, defeated by age, for enigmatic reasons assigned to the chess delegation sent to Geneva. The rest were two or three men appointed as his escorts: the indispensable Komarov, permanent candidate to the title (he couldn't be trusted: Leontiev had systematically dashed his attempts at the crown), and Heifetz, good old Heifetz, a Jew from Odessa who supervised the champion's training and helped analyze each game, or the unexpected defeats.

At noon he found Heifetz, as usual, in the hotel's dining room, at the table reserved for the Soviet delegation. He looked more concerned than on other instances, his face poorly shaven. He was going through the notes taken the day before during the inaugural match.

"I hope that the African didn't disturb your sleep, Isaac," said the champion, approaching and waving at the waiter.

Heifetz smiled nonchalantly.

"Appetite and sleep, Nikolai."

"It's not that serious, my friend."

"Yet rather disconcerting," insisted Heifetz, "You must have realized that his game is not an example of orthodoxy."

"Neither is mine, don't you think? Any chess innovation ends up by becoming, sooner or later, a matter of orthodoxy, Issac. It's like the revolution: first the Winter Palace must be stormed, then some order must be reinstated, the new rules established. This doesn't rob it of originality."

"Of course not. I meant that the African has his own rules, his own method. That move in which he immediately pushes the king forward, moving it between the pawns... it's sheer madness!"

"That has given him excellent results for the time being. Pure improvisation, Heifetz, don't fool yourself. He might have learned three or four tricks in his Mauritanian village and he applied them yesterday with great luck."

"And now he has one advantage point over us."

"It doesn't matter. My line of pawns will put him in his place tomorrow."

"Anyhow, it would be wise to review the game."

Leontiev shrugged his shoulders. It was unnecessary. Yesterday's game was stamped in his mind in every detail, every move after the opening—pawn to king four—,that the African reproduced, until in one stroke he wrecked all orthodoxy and brought forth the arrogant figure of his king, setting him in the place the pawn had vacated. That was undoubtedly a surprise, to bring the king forth on the second move during a contest for the title! Somebody should warn Prince Kane that this was not a hunt for rhinoceros, if there are any rhinos in Mauritania. Apart from the forever malnourished human population.

The rest was just as perplexing. The African rapidly got rid of several pawns while Leontiev, still hopeful, clung to his own. On the other hand, nobody expected anything from Kane but that he simply fulfill his role with dignity. Heifetz and Marshall Shukov were bewildered when from the start of the ninth move the African's queen found her way through the pawn ranks of the Soviet champion and started to decimate his rear guard: first a bishop, taken in exchange for nothing, and after that it was impossible to neutralize that advantage. Leontiev made a last effort by attacking with his pawns, but he was shamefully despoiled by his adversary's queen and bishops. He didn't even get to step on the palace's front staircase with his army of ragged dispossessed. At the end of four miserable hours, he had to face the facts. Grabbing his own king by the neck he threw him face down at the feet of the Mauritanian.

Just a simple slip, no more, no less than that. As the *Frankfurter Allgemeine* pointed out that morning, "A bad day for the Soviet champion." The special correspondent concluded in his summation of the match, "A moment of distraction during the ninth move and the African slipped in, without warning, through the center in an irresistible attack, bringing unexpected glory to the black continent and no less disgrace to old Russia. There will be better things at the final matches. The Soviets' Leontiev is a hard bone to gnaw and he has demonstrated this during almost thirty years of undisputed reign."

Of course, thought Leontiev, flattered. He had demonstrated it, but with one correction: his was not a monarchy, rather a republic protected by the strength and vigor of the humble, those who had nothing to lose but their chains, the most numerous, determined since times immemorial to rid themselves of those who wore powdered wigs and exhibited such good manners on the chessboard.

Relying on this conviction he waited for the coming day (he was pained to notice that the number of fans requesting his autograph at the hotel door had dwindled by half) and prepared to arrive on time at the Hunter's Hall of the Angleterre. This time Kane was waiting for him on stage in an attitude of deep concentration, staring at the chess pieces, his elbows resting at the edge of the chessboard.

"Just a slip," thought Leontiev. "He is only a black with good luck."

There were not many lucky blacks, but this one at least seemed sure of his own good fortune. During the second game he once again advanced the king and then the queen. This time things turned out even worse than at the first match. A flank assault by the queen and the bishops from the opponent prompted the baffled Soviet champion to concentrate his scrawny pawns in the center of the chessboard in a disorganized fashion, only to see them helplessly reduced in number, once more without the adequate compensations. Increased dismay spread silently among the audience at each new move from the African. Two hours after the start of the match, Kane had the situation well under control and smiled nonchalantly to the spectators.

"A Masai," thought Leontiev. "A Masai with the airs of an aristocrat who prefers to risk everything on the queen."

When the first check came about, he only managed to retreat. The few pawns left were of little help. The surviving bishop and the prestigious "Leontiev defense" were reduced to a handful of dispersed pieces and deserters who desperately sought to leave the chessboard at the cry of each new check, badly mispronounced by the African. Scarcely three hours into the fight, Leontiev thought that he perceived a definite sign. For the hundredth time, one of his pawns remained within range of the rival's knight without a chance of escape. His face covered with sweat, obviously congested, the Soviet contender evoked the most memorable incident in his childhood, the story his mother used to repeat at night: the attack by the "white" Russians and the Cossacks against the areas surrounding Kiev, when his father was annihilated under the hooves of the enemy.

"Check," said the African once more.

An unnecessary announcement. Leontiev had just risen from his chair, stretching out his hand in a contrived congratulatory gesture, thus putting an end to the second match.

***

There was an excellent asparagus soup and roast beef, but nobody was in the mood to appreciate good cooking. The Marshall noisily sipped the wine and the soup. The rest ingested lunch in the strictest silence. Heifetz showed a slight tremor of the chin, probably fearful of a sudden *pogrom* by some members of the delegation. By dessert they were speaking about the weather and the traditional individualism of the Swiss.

"It isn't that serious," Leontiev finally said to approach the matter preying on everybody's mind. "It can still be corrected."

Only Komarov, the permanent understudy from Sebastopol, dared contradict him.

"With two points against? This is not a neighborhood contest in Stalingrad, Nikolai. It isn't wise to allow so much advantage in a match for the title."

"Exactly what I expected from you, Komarov. A word of encouragement!"

"I only hope that you decide to play in earnest, champion."

"Please, gentlemen," interjected Shukov. "This is no time for a quarrel."

"Perhaps if we analyze the games," suggested Heifetz shyly.

"There is no time for it," said the Marshall. "There is more at stake than a few tricks and technicalities on the chessboard."

"My defense system is far more than that," stated Leontiev, offended. "Or doesn't anybody trust my pawns anymore?"

"It doesn't matter anymore, Nikolai. Just win the remaining games with the pawns or the king. I couldn't care less which."

"I do care!" replied the champion impatiently.

"Why?"

"It's a matter of principle. Things are different when you are on the stage."

"I know that," the Marshall approved without hesitation. "I have spent many years on stage. What matters is to stay on it, Nikolai. Who cares how you do it? With the queen or the king, at this point you don't have much to lose."

"My prestige, Marshall."

"I will see that your prestige is restored when we return to Moscow with the title in our hands."

Leontiev observed him in dismay. He finished the dessert in silence.

That evening he roamed alone again—except for the body-guards—walking by the edge of the lake. The first shadows of dusk again found him pensive at the little square dedicated to Rousseau, who still smiled on his stone monolith. Was it that simple then? Just a question of shelving his tactics, a whole life relying on the pawns, to substitute them now, from one minute to the next, with the queen or the king? After having kept the crown for almost three decades? To finally surrender to the army of wretched courtiers that this Kane, monarch of the rabble born in the most miserable corner of Africa, had managed to manipulate skillfully during the first two games?

It was already dark when he saw him. His rival had just reached the Pont des Bergues, stopping by the railing a few meters from the square to contemplate idly the lake's surface, a ferry filled with tourists, and the gigantic water jet in the distance.

From his improvised hiding place among the benches, Leontiev examined him thoroughly, yielding to an irrepressible curiosity.

"What a monarch," he thought, searching the darkness of his face and the occasional gleam of his implacable teeth. "King of nothing, at the most a few girls with pendulous breasts." He didn't even have time to inwardly celebrate his unsuspected anthropological considerations. The African tourist on the bridge—nobody would guess that he was the candidate for the title—had just fixed his gaze on the square and Rousseau's monolith now immersed in shadows, simultaneously discovering Leontiev among the trees and hedges, and observed him for a few seconds from his inconceivable height and his darkness. And then Kane smiled at him with a smattering of cordiality in his shining features, like the distant brightness of a bonfire in the forest.

Leontiev didn't know if he should respond to his gesture or pretend not to notice, fraternize or ignore him, the only two alternatives. He opted to leave the bench, turning his back. He breathed deeply and left the small garden with the bodyguards following him.

He walked the right bank of the lake until very late. In the proximity of the railroad station and the Place Cornavin, he verified the presence of other Africans on the streets, all of them dressed in orange garb, the uniform that city hall gave them to meticulously sweep the sidewalks of Geneva. No detectable signs of royalty among them, no bonfires or lances, just the distant and penetrating gaze, the same traces of haughtiness that

Prince Anibal Kane used when staring at him during the games, like a Masai warrior watching his prey.

* * *

Once again it was his turn to initiate the match, once again he had been favored with the white pieces. Shukov and Heifetz watched him from the first row, obviously tense and expectant. He didn't even have to ponder the alternatives. Since last night he knew what would happen. He remembered an evening long ago in Stalingrad, the bewildered look on the face of the young defeated partisan, the Cossack's hooves over his father's horrified face.

He immediately searched the ranks of his army with index and thumb. He hesitated for just a second and then grabbed the king, the white sovereign who now marched forth among his subjects, appearing arrogantly at the palace staircase, anticipating from that vantage point the imminent attack from his black adversaries, the line of pawns—yes, now the pawns—that the Mauritanian started to put in motion toward the staircase. Nothing further to add, except for a last desperate grand gesture from the white prince and his retinue, while the African multiplied his pawns around him, harassing him once more, springing up from all directions, from the undergrowth, the jungle, amidst the growing rumble of the tom-tom in the night, a rhythmic background of voices and ritual shrieks, an explosion of merriment and dancing, blurred faces in the surrounding thickets, stalking the white sovereign who now tried to slither away with his lady and the battered remnants of his army, seeking refuge at the end of the chessboard and waiting there for the definitive blow...

It scarcely lasted two hours. Shortly after six, Nikolai Leontiev made the last move of his career and his king entered with no fanfare and little conviction into the only square to which he was entitled.

"Check!" said the African, and smiled for one last time, with an air of condescension.

an empty cage

I arrived at the Schönbrunn zoo, where I now live, by conventional means with a horde of French, two or three Scandinavians, possibly a German, several dozen Japanese whose faces, all of them, I now see multiplied with some individual variations along the gravel paths of this enclosure. The visit to the Imperial Palace, just a few meters from the zoo, lasted a little over one hour. It was an exhaustive run through the Hapsburgs' depressing halls where the Austro-Hungarian empress occasionally used to seek refuge with her innumerable progeny—Marie Antoinette among them the least fortunate of her offspring, who would crown her everlasting vanity under the guillotine. To be or not to be, of course, is the only authentic dilemma.

It's difficult to explain why I stayed at Schönbrunn. I can't think of another reason except my first, acute vision of the primates and an accumulation of unexpected considerations that led me to abandon the line of tourists, which at the time was weaving past the orangutan's cage. It was there, in a somber and damp place, in the section reserved for simians, where everything changed, when I literally felt entranced by the orangutan and his disheveled, indomitable mane. A spectacle that made me stop, obstructing the monochord flow of the visitors who took advantage of this circumstance to insult me in German and Japanese. That was the precise instant of alienation, the unforeseen flight onward. The orangutan, nesting nonchalantly among the tallest branches of a tree, watched us serenely, detached from the heterogeneous parade of visitors who ambled by the cage's bars, people willing to spend a year's savings going through cathedrals and palaces, from one zoo to another, while a stoic Japanese tries to find with his telephoto lens the most photogenic angle of the orangutan, that "corrupt replica of man," the medieval scholastics suggested. But it is well known that for those inhabitants of the abbeys everything was a failed act of the divinity.

The visit ended for me right there, lost in contemplation of the orangutan, who in turn observed me with intense curiosity, all of his senses concentrated in deciphering my humble being. At that moment I fancied that everything was really reversed, that the corrupt replica of the divine humorist was ourselves, the visitors ambling by the cage, the grotesque crowd swarming around me on this side of the cage's bars while the orangutan watched us from his enviable freedom from the other side, indifferent to our gestures and postures, watching us with his mocking eyes, the same impudent expression he exhibits whenever I return to his ambit, undressing me with his stare, strengthening in me the conviction that everything was, is, exactly reversed. And the cage is ours.

That day I decided to stay in Schönbrunn.

***

The same night I settled down in the vicinity of the pit where giraffes and tapirs dwell, the "impar-hoofed mammals" (as the annex placard reads), and the so-called "artiodactyls," those with double or quadruple hoofs; the camel, the deer, the Nepalese ox. I built my hiding place there, a cave made out of rotting planks and bales of straw, after carefully pondering the most probable route that the zoo employees would follow. In view of the obvious neglect of the surroundings, I surmised that they seldom went into that area. I wasn't wrong. They limited themselves to deliver some bales for each cage now and then and the site's inhabitants continued that way, undisturbed in their gastronomic routine, ruminating all day, chewing that diet exempt of all novelty.

I organized my dwelling at the back of the site assigned to the giraffes, who gradually became used to my presence after treating themselves to a few furtive nibbles from my thatch roof, initially reticent with the new guest in Schönbrunn, a specimen lodged without authorization from anyone in the proximity of their cage, still dressed in his civilian rags, filthy and muddy, although even now enslaved to his few possessions, the bed of leaves and newspapers on which I lay every night, a comb I don't use anymore but keep for indecipherable reasons as a symbolic hindrance from the past to prove (to whom?) that at one time I was—me, the beggar of Schönbrunn—an honorable citizen.

I fed myself, naturally, in a sporadic fashion, once in a while biting fearfully into the meat and vegetables that I managed to steal from a cage, except those of the felines, to avoid becoming an involuntary substitute for their usual diet. The zoo employees distributed the food at noon. A strange habit on their part, as though a leopard or a boar should follow the digestive patterns of humans. I know that they disliked seeing me roaming with obvious avidity around the containers of meat and fruit, fish for the seals, carrots and vegetables for the primates. Even when I was hiding among the bushes, they sensed my odorous presence and made comments in German, laughing uproariously until they discovered me crouching in their vicinity. Some of them would grab a stick, the rest surrounded me howling, laughing, supported by the rules and regulations of the zoo, ordering me to come out of the bushes and leave the place, staggering from malnutrition, empty-handed.

I had nothing left but the slim chance of finding leftover food in the cages, some greens and vegetables snatched from the chimpanzees or a tame macaque from North Africa, two or three coaitas monkeys who shared their cage with a green monkey from Senegal, for whom they cared little: sometimes they all ganged up on him for a beating or stealthily grabbed him by the tail. It's quite understandable; it's not every day that someone can enjoy the company of a monkey of inconceivable coloring, impudent in his histrionics and green pride.

This was also, more or less, what my presence provoked among the coaitas-employees of the zoo, always ready to wield a club, particularly a red-haired, hefty lad with a slobbering facial expression. On one occasion I decided to confront them.

I had headed early to my den, but my uniformed adversaries had, for the hundredth time, destroyed it and one of the giraffes was calmly chewing on the remains. Desperate, without thinking about what I was doing, I ran to the offices at the zoo's entrance where they all met in the evening on the terrace for a cup of tea before going home.

Keeping a safe distance from their tables, I raised my arm and my voice.

"Very well!" I said. "You must be happy now! You have satisfied your wish for impossible redemption once more, you coaitas of the devil! Go on, feed the giraffes with my walls, destroy my home again, you grotesque messengers of the authorities, miserable puppets of scheduled labor, full-time jackasses with limited ambitions! Raze my refuge again, archangels of nothing, slaves to weekends and miserable salaries! Repeat ad infinitum the ceremony of disintegration, devour my newspaper bed, burn my beams, let everything slowly rot! With my hands I shall rebuild everything in another place in this zoo, I shall once again build my home, and yet again, and return to it at night to shield myself from your rancor!"

There was no answer. They all remained motionless, jaws dropped, the tea cups suspended in their hands. Finally the red-haired lad with the slobbering expression got up from his chair and went into the building, probably to fetch a club. I opted not to wait for confirmation.

The next day they were all angry, which had repercussions on the residents of the zoo. The coaitas doubled the usual doses of slaps to the green interloper, and two sea lions started a match of reciprocal bites and fin slapping early in the morning. One of the employees got mixed up with the rations, spilling several tubs of fish in the rhesus macaque's cage. I considered the prevailing confusion as my personal triumph.

That first phase of my stay in Schönbrunn was not particularly easy to bear. Winter slowly undermined my health. Once in a while I would dream of returning to the city and immersing myself in the opera again, to vibrate with some of Puccini's emotional calamities or a priceless solo by Ruggiero Raimondi in the penumbra of the Staatsoper. And perhaps settle again in a comfortable Viennese dwelling, protected from the city, tramways, bankers and street musicians. I found solace in thinking that Diogenes lived in a barrel in the markets of Athens and his meager diet didn't transcend the leftovers he could secure at the end of the day. That neither he could accomplish the return trip.

At rutting time, when the primates and the rest of the zoo's inhabitants felt the urge to ostentatiously display their genital attributes and utter the howling that encourages desire, everything became more tolerable. At such a time I roamed in the vicinity of the vast place assigned to the mandrills, a cement platform surrounded by a pit filled with the cloudy and foamy waters that receive the simians' wastes and simultaneously—nothing is done without a purpose at Schönbrunn—protects them from the crowd. That's where the collective ritual took place, a copulatory symphony that the males sang astride the females, spreading surprise and bafflement among the visitors of the zoo. More than one kid entitled himself to a slap because of his insistence on sticking close to the enclosure's bars.

Anyhow, none of this reduced the wantonness and unrestrained passion of the mandrills, or the ceremony enacted by two or three males who gained the most advantage, tacitly dividing territory and the more numerous females among themselves. The copulating was brief and devoid of preambles. Surrounded by his retinue, the male waited until the reddish instrument jutted out between his legs, thus announcing his readiness for pleasure. One of the females decided then to come near (how did they assign turns, what unsuspected hierarchy determined the privilege of being first?), offering her behind, that callused, red, bald portion of her anatomy. The male would couple himself to her with an air of aloofness, both crouching down, and put an end to the proceedings in a few seconds, suddenly separating to return to their individuality soaked in sun and parasites.

By evening I was returning to my hiding place to free my hands from any urban habit and allow them to stray down toward my crotch, my breathing labored, listening attentively to the moans and groans of the beasts in the distance while the day was coming to an end in Schönbrunn's gardens, amid the croaking of a bird in some remote corner and the constant ruminating of the giraffes in the adjoining cage, from tapir and zebras likewise, an irreplaceable melody that preceded the night like a delicate backdrop to my panting in time to feverish massaging of my instrument in the shadows of my cave.

But no problem lasts a hundred years, they say, and the exposure to the elements, the harassment by the coaitas-employees, were not an exception to this blessed rule that frees us of the worst misfortunes. I found it at the end of winter, in April, when I wandered into unknown areas of the zoo, into the section assigned to flamingoes and ducks, swans and quails, all piled together in a fenced pond on the east side of the zoo. There I discovered the subterfuge I had been longing for. It looked as though abandoned for several years; the bars were covered with rust. There was a listless tree in the center, gnawed by termites and freezing temperatures. An empty cage! An empty cage in the heart of Schönbrunn!

It happened by successive visits with the spring's arrival. A few days later I returned to the area to confirm that it was still there. Somebody, perhaps one of the senior employees, had the courtesy to open the side door for me one day, like a promise whispered in my ear, and one sunny Sunday in May I vaulted into the cage.

That night I slept curled up by the trunk of the tree. On the following days I wandered through the neighboring areas. Not far from my place I found a small wood board. With a piece of charcoal I wrote on it: "Mammal of the subspecies Eutheria. Warm blood" and hung it on the bars in view of the public. One of the employees remarked to me later, when he brought my food, that the bit about "warm blood" was redundant.

The next day a Japanese and two Italians came to take my first pictures.

the lost years*

Nothing extraordinary. The deaths of Bruno and the Englishman sealed, as expected, something that came up in the opposite field, that gap in the habitual routine where unexpected options converge, the exaggerated gestures, the exceptions that, much to our chagrin, confirm the rule. For both of them there will be no more exceptions, just the anonymity of the common grave beneath a wooden cross and a succinct epitaph: "No name, died in unknown circumstances, May 1980." Even at the time, when somebody facetiously submitted the idea of an abduction, we all toyed with the realistic possibility of an end and an honorable death to finalize with some degree of heroism a stratagem devised in great detail at Bruno's house. Then we reached the foreseeable outcome that we all sensed intuitively, even before stepping into the Santiago metro and demanding immediate transportation to Cuba in one of its cars as a deliberate parody of something that, taking advantage of other means of transportation, had become a habitual news item in the world press. A possibility that could only end in a shoot-out and spilled blood, with two of our own abandoned on the underground tracks and the rest of us behind bars.

A sudden agreement on the absurdity of the plan and its refreshing possibilities was the origin of it all. The month of May was calmly evolving, but just the mention of May unexpectedly opened the way to the most intense of excitements. Somebody brought to mind the effervescent events of '68 in Paris and the French capital sporting black and red flags, posters and graffiti everywhere and Cohn-Bendit in Nanterre urging the French to leave their apartments or their four-cylinder Renaults and get out onto the streets to scream at the

* This short story won the 1985 "Ciudad de Villena" award in Alicante, Spain.

top of their lungs, to cover the republican guards with a mantle of cobblestones and briefly unite against the established order, the mob rising against the establishment. It had happened about ten years earlier but it still throbbed emotionally in us, in any place on the globe: the collective desire to repeat those events, the naive belief that we could shake the dust off the banners to rock the present scenario again. The Englishman had been in Paris in '68 and could see the consequences of all that more clearly than we could. With our unlimited loyalty to Lenin and his watered-down prescriptions, it was difficult for us to imagine that the apparently innocuous act of writing slogans on public restroom walls (the one about "The tyrant wears long johns," or other slightly more offensive options), or walking in an inebriated euphoria on top of parked cars (one of us tried something like this one evening, mostly because he was drunk), could be the seed of an entirely new concept in the worn out primer of revolutionary practice.

Upon reconsidering the events of '68 and Hugo's fit of rage that prompted him to climb over a parked car and walk all over it, proclaiming from his just-acquired higher stature that "the time for pedestrians has arrived," in a surprising flash of collective inspiration we came upon the underground train, the impeccable Santiago metro, which was also a French undertaking, a revealing coincidence with our newly defined goal: the unexpected abduction of one of its cars and the demand, equally unexpected, at the time of negotiations, for our transportation to Havana as our final destination. "There is method to their madness," somebody had written on a wall in Nanterre, with a reference to Hamlet, and that is exactly what it was: the time had come to cross the threshold of sanity. Madness and the grotesque should come forth, if only to confuse the enemy for a few hours.

Samuel was the most stubbornly opposed to the whole scheme. Once everything was arranged at Bruno's house and the weapons were ready (three AK rifles and two revolvers, plus the respective ammunition), he gravely warned us of the risks and disadvantages of "insurrectional focus," a stage already left behind with Guevara and the Peredos' failed attempt in Bolivia.

And, of course, he was right. A single swallow doesn't make a summer, and we didn't need much intelligence to anticipate the kick in the ass, at the least, that each one of us would get. In spite of it all, nobody—not even Samuel—seriously considered the possibility of deserting. Perhaps the initiative—now considered quite disreputable—of starting an uprising on our own remained alive within us, each one willing to live his very personal heroic moment and laugh uproariously at the wolf's fangs after having avoided its horrifying slashes for years.

At the time it was not a matter of waiting for the generals to generously restore our civil rights. It was not a question of boarding the metro again in the regular fashion after submissively buying a ticket, running it through the slot and pushing the gate, yielding without aggravation or reflection to a brief wait and the tedium of the daily trip, going through the gestures of the most detestable urbanity every day—by all means, you go first—feeling that life oozed away into every tunnel and turn of a trajectory designed by Frenchmen, gradually losing the most precarious notion of freedom and improvisation. Knowing we were programmed, always following a straight line, reduced to the condition of a mere gear in that universe of wan faces, tardy citizens and blinding lights, until we become easy prey to memories, until suddenly we become aware of the depths we are treading and corroborate that there, in the abyss, underground and whereabouts unknown, thousands of men and women lay—abducted from their homes during the nights of the military uprising years ago. And in the ensuing months, several years of raids and kidnappings, tubs filled with excrement, wanton beatings, the blows that were impossible to avoid while wearing a permanent blindfold, insults and humiliations, electric shocks to breasts and testicles, each nightly hostage lost in the caverns of the new order, torn by torture, fragmented in body and spirit, meticulously abused only to finally disappear and be eliminated without a trace in the bowels of the city at the same level as the tracks that the underground train traveled every morning. Which we couldn't board conventionally anymore due to the sting of our bad conscience and the pending debts. At that juncture it was more honorable to walk well armed into the tunnel and force the engineer to stop, if only to pay silent homage to all those who lay lost underground for so many years.

***

Horacio joined the crowd at the last minute, with everybody's consent, although we didn't clearly know why. Perhaps because of his own foolishness—a fact supported by several diagnoses—that contributed to further legitimize an initiative prompted in the last analysis by his own suggestion, born from the mischief he inhabited since adolescence. He had deserted then the universe of reason amid the fiery reactions that any move of that kind sparks in the nucleus of a family with a penchant for good manners. Horacio had refused to submit, reducing to a minimum the frequency of his hygienic rituals, at the same time refusing to work or comply with other "administrative impositions"—as he said—initiating a memorable relationship with a mutt known as "Charlie," to whom he confided his sorrows and worries, waiting for a revealing bark, until the dog catcher took him away. As recommended, the family called on several specialists without any positive results. Nothing—not even medications or periodic electric shocks—could bring him to normality. Now he arrogantly paraded his delirium in the streets of Santiago, except when the family decided to institutionalize him once more to mitigate his crimes. When he was free he slept in old, crumbling inns and occasionally visited the friends who still remained loyal—the same that now pondered the possibility of shunning him and fleeing to Cuba—to request with unabashed directness a dish of food or a sympathetic ear. The first was granted promptly, the latter he had to fight for, tooth and nail.

A few days before the abduction, the Englishman and I found him at the Catholic University station where we were going over the terrain. A strange mixture of a penultimate tramp and a first stowaway on the flight to Venus, he came up on the platform flaunting his untidy appearance, hidden behind his spectacles and wrapped in the gray coat he had inherited from his grandfather. But this time there was something different, a peculiarity in his clothing that inevitably caught our attention in spite of our being used to his eccentricities: he wasn't wearing trousers. Under the ragged coat his naked shins showed unashamedly over the old, muddy shoes, in plain view of the public. He stopped dead in his tracks when he saw us near him. He smiled with the delight of a shipwrecked man who finally sees a boat on the horizon and joined us in two long strides.

"Blessed are the eyes that look at you!" he solemnly proclaimed, "and he who rediscovers beneath the city the comrades of endless hours that the greedy calendar will never return to us!"

This was followed by affectionate back slapping and hugging, as he did every time we ran into each other. He had been released from the hospital for the hundredth time, he explained.

"Which allows me to transport my anatomy from one end to the other of this city without qualms, this being the only relevant thing to do, my brothers, I need not stress the point."

"Even if you don't eat?" I remarked, noticing that he was thinner than the last time I had seen him.

"Even if I don't eat. But the bread that I only occasionally manage to get now is in any case better than the electricity they feed me at the hospital, man. They must think I'm a fluorescent bulb, the sons of bitches."

"What happened to your trousers?"

He looked at his bare shins in puzzlement, as though searching his memory for a probable cause of his sudden nakedness.

"It was an accident," he concluded, "that has now and then forced me to spend the night in several police stations of this ignoble city, under the reiterated allegation that I offend the morals and good habits of the citizenry."

"They stole your trousers?"

"Not exactly. It was some time ago in a hostel. One day I woke up at dawn with a strange feeling. A premonition. And of course, the old man in the adjoining bed was already up getting his belongings together. Among them he had included my trousers, carefully purloined during the night from my belongings to cover his rickety legs. So I jumped from my bed and expressed my dissatisfaction, with one or two punches and a variety of curses... I don't know why."

A shadow of unmistakable sadness crossed his face at that moment.

"As a sole answer to my imprecations," he continued, "the old man started to snivel. That was the worst of it."

"What did he do?" asked the Englishman.

"He started to cry, man, like a Mary Magdalene." Horacio stopped a minute to ponder. "At that instant I realized that that man's soul was no doubt as ragged and full of holes as my trousers. And I don't know why I remembered my grandfather. That man was my grandfather alive again for a few seconds, standing before me as I awakened, with the same desolation in his face as just before he departed this damned world. A broken old man, brothers, half stooped and poorer than me. How much misfortune stood facing me that morning! A man at his wits' end, no more, no less."

"And you gave him your trousers."

"Of course. After letting down my guard and crying wordlessly with him for a while, I suggested he leave the premises, going to hell if he so choose and take my trousers with him... I remained trembling in the darkness until dawn's light appeared. Afterward I donned this fine cashmere garment inherited from my grandfather and went out into the street. At noon the cops grabbed me the first time. It wouldn't be the last... But it's not important, brothers. Proudhon already said it: property is theft. I don't know, until winter comes to this den of misery, I see no point in looking up the old man and beating him up again...which he deserves, don't you think?"

There was a pause. The Englishman and I remained pensive, watching him intently. He had just stepped into another dimension. His gaze wandered to a distant place, while he smiled at the void, probably at his grandfather's ghost or at "Charlie" who occasionally came to visit him from the recesses of memory. There wasn't much to add. His shins shone with unexpected meaning, a luminosity that the Englishman and I hadn't noticed until then. In his nonchalant manner Horacio represented in the streets, even then, the frustrated dream of those who, unlike him, had already renounced the cobblestones as projectiles. In a way his naked shins were far more meaning-ful than all of Marcuse or the perishable harangues from Cohn-Bendit in Nanterre. He was the missing man.

"Would you like to go to Cuba, Horacio?" the Englishman and I asked, almost simultaneously.

***

At an early hour on Tuesday, all six of us left our headquar-ters heading toward our objective. Three of us carried a myste-riously elongated and obviously heavy plastic bag. Dressed from head to toe for the occasion, Horacio reminded us some-what worriedly that it was Tuesday and "on Tuesday neither marry nor start a journey, as the proverb clearly states." The meeting place was the Catholic University station where we walked in separate contingents to avoid creating suspicion among the passersby. Bruno and I walked from Lastarria toward the Alameda, the rest along an adjoining street. If everything worked as expected, our arrivals at the chosen station would coincide within no more than a matter of minutes.

The city was quietly stirring to activity. We walked in silence, to the rhythm of sleepy men and women, until we arrived at the Alameda and found ourselves abruptly facing the access to the underground metro.

"The time has come," said Bruno, descending the stairs. "Next stop, the Caribbean."

The rest of us were already on the platform, mixing in casually with the crowd of habitual travelers. Samuel was the most relaxed, in spite of his reluctance about the project. Horacio, on the other hand, seemed ready to join a charge of the light brigade.

The train, consisting of five cars, arrived within a few seconds and opened its doors with the usual creaking sound. The Englishman and other conspirators stepped separately into the four rear coaches, each responsible for one. Bruno and I stepped into the one with the conductor. Once it started moving again, I made a quick visual survey of the passengers, our eventual hostages: about twenty persons—an old man with a tired expression, several men who looked like bank employees, two schoolgirls, a few women and two or three laborers.

The train had now entered the tunnel. Bruno signaled me with his eyes that the time for action had arrived and I advanced toward the conductor's booth. My hand was shaking when I opened the door. The conductor turned around surprised and explained the rules to me.

"You are not supposed to come in here, my friend."

"I think I am, my friend," I answered, drawing my revolver. "This is a kidnapping and for the time being you don't have the right to ask questions." The man instinctively reduced the speed. "Continue driving, don't stop! At the next station stop as though everything is all right, and then wait until I tell you what to do."

We were fast approaching the Baquedano station that proceeds east, whose lights were blinking in the distance, coming steadily toward us. Here Bruno would retain the first car's passengers. The Englishman and the rest would empty the remaining wagons.

From behind the door to the booth I heard Bruno, fully mastering his leader's role, explaining the situation to the passengers.

"This is a hijacking, ladies and gentlemen. If you cooperate with us there will be no problems. Be kind enough to stay in your seats. Nobody will leave this car at the next stop."

As expected, this prompted an explosion of questions and outrage that quickly faded into silence when the plastic wrapping that my colleague carried abruptly turned into an AK-47.

The train entered Baquedano station at the usual speed. On the platform about a dozen passengers waited to board, a futile hope that the Englishman and the others proceeded to dispel.

After the regular stop, the passengers' grumbling on board reached the cabin, mostly from those urged to step out as in a stampede from the last four cars. The loudest protests were from the women, while Hugo and Samuel's voices overwhelmed the crowd. "Everybody out, no complaining! You can't come in, sir, for reasons of national security!"

Events developed more smoothly than expected. Seconds later I got the signal from Bruno indicating that the evacuation proceedings had ended.

"Now we leave," I ordered the conductor. "Close the doors and leave, fast!"

The train left the station nearly empty. Only the passengers from the first car remained on board. Entering the tunnel once more, the conductor recovered his power of speech.

"I think that you are making a mistake," he suggested. "Because if what you want is money, there ain't any here."

"Everything in good time, my friend. Besides that's not it, don't worry. Money doesn't bring happiness." We were half way between Baquedano and Salvador, the next station. "Stop now!"

"Here in the tunnel?"

"Yes, right here."

The train came to a standstill in a darkness broken here and there by a string of phosphorescent lights. The abduction plan ended there. Now we would enter the phase of public relations.

"O.K.," I said, "now call headquarters and tell them to stop the rest of the trains. We are leaving for Cuba."

The man was obviously puzzled. He stared at me. He tried to smile.

"Where did you say you are going?"

"Cuba."

"Cuba?"

"That's right."

"In the metro?"

"In the metro."

This time the pause was longer.

"Let me see," he concluded. "You mean to…?"

"The Caribbean. You must have heard it mentioned some time."

"Yes, of course."

"Well, that's it," I ratified. "In the Caribbean."

"I know that but… it's impossible."

"You call headquarters, and that's all. It's not your problem."

"But it's…it's an island. A piece of land surrounded by water."

"We know that," I explained. "Now make that call. Tell

them what's going on before the next train crashes into us."
The reaction at headquarters was foreseeable. In the first
place they refused to stop the other trains' circulation, threatening to fire the conductor and applying various sanctions against
him, repeatedly making references to his mother of whom they
apparently had a poor opinion. Later, more attuned to the
situation, they asked him exactly what was involved, how many
of us were on board and the size of our arsenal, what did we look
like, if any of us was drooling steadily and what other symptoms
of lunacy were detectable. In a serious and steady voice I
explained the hostages' situation to headquarters through the
microphone: twenty passengers were kept on board the head
car. It was advisable to heed our demands or face the consequences. At this point the voice from headquarters faded out
and I heard an order addressed to another official. "Stop all
trains. Advise everybody that we have a problem." Then the
engineer at headquarters started talking again.
"This is a joke, isn't it?"
"No, sir."
"But...do you realize what you are asking for? It's an
island, a piece of land surrounded by water," he reiterated with
evident lack of originality. "Why don't you hijack a plane or a
ship instead?"
"We get airsick easily."
At this point the man lost patience.
"Where do you all come from, tell me? Did they give you
a day free from the psychiatric hospital and you decided to leave
for Cuba on the metro, is that it?"
"Not exactly. Anyway, don't lose your cool. It's too early
for that."
"Is that what you think? You force me to paralyze the whole
underground system in Santiago and ask me not to lose my
cool? Let me tell you something..."
"I'm listening."
"We don't travel to Cuba. We can't comply with your
demand, I'm sorry. Now stop this shit and let us get on with our
job in peace, right?"
"No."

I heard a deep, long sigh on the microphone and then the man started to talk sense.

"All right, I'll have to inform the Department of the Interior," he said.

The rest is history and in the newspapers. Several hours of negotiations extending till early morning Wednesday were enough for the palace's high command to summon their bloodhounds and save the cost of forcible transportation to the Caribbean.

During this time the train remained idle in the tunnel's darkness, which allowed some fraternization with the hostages, eight men and eleven women, not counting the conductor. At first we demanded that they all stay in their seats, right there in the first car. After a couple of hours a woman complained of leg cramps and Bruno allowed the hostages to walk between the seats, which reduced the tension naturally created at the sight of our weapons. Somebody asked what had led us to hijack the metro and not a plane or invade an embassy. This question cautiously reflected the same concern expressed by the engineer at headquarters. It was supposed to determine whether we were a group of lunatics or any similar possibility. Horacio somehow contributed to the first hypothesis after he perched himself outside the train and attacked an old song by Bob Dylan at full throttle. The two schoolgirls stuck their heads out a door to listen to the rather strenuous rendition of the ballad by our improvised troubadour.

Nobody had answered the question. "The answer, my friend, is blowing in the wind," Horacio was now singing. The truth is that nothing could justify what was happening. To explain at that point that, all things considered, there was a method to our madness, would not have helped clarify matters. The conductor, who seemed anxious to recover some of his authority, also wanted to know whether we really planned to kill them, a legitimate concern that sparked a great deal of worry among the passengers.

"Not at all," affirmed Bruno. "We are here because we want to go to Cuba. That's why we are detaining you."

"And if they refuse to take you there?" The conductor

persisted.

"We shall wait to see what develops. In any case we are not going to shoot you. You may relax."

This is how Bruno expressed the group's authentic intentions. Because, truly, nobody was willing to pull a trigger against those people. Under any circumstances.

Finally at four the conductor from headquarters put us in touch by radio with a representative from the Department of the Interior, a colonel something-or-other. Bruno brooded over the news that our demands "were being thoroughly analyzed by the qualified authorities." Before hanging up, we requested food and some beverages because the hostages were hungry. We were told that the demand "would be carefully considered by the qualified authorities," and that they would call back in one hour.

By that time the hostages had asked permission to smoke, which was granted without hesitation by the third in charge on the train—the Englishman. Upon our return from the booth, Bruno and I were asked about the food.

"They are studying the matter," I replied. "They will call back once they've come to a decision."

This was received with jeers and various protests. As usual, the stomach was the first symptom of popular discontent.

Later, the situation became a sort of picnic, which was nothing to laugh about, for sure, but nobody was in the mood to make things worse by uttering irrelevant threats. Really, nobody seemed to know which attitudes and behavior were stipulated under such circumstances. The women chatted among themselves about the tasks pending at their offices or their bosses' neuroses. The schoolgirls talked with Horacio, demanding that he repeat some of the songs in his repertoire. Unaccustomed to such laudable interest in his vocal talents, our friend happily agreed, embellishing the kidnapping with an unscheduled musical background that brought forth the risk of his continuing his performance for the rest of the day.

Hugo took over the responsibility of the occasional cases of elemental biological needs, alternately escorting the hostages outside the car to an area from which the inevitable human aromas already permeated the atmosphere.

The male hostages were the most cautious and as a whole remained silent and angry, although none of them had expressed a desire to return to civilization through the tunnel—not even when, by our leader's extremely praiseworthy statement, they learned that we had no intention of shooting them down.

The one who worried us was the conductor. His loyalty to the company or to his colleagues could not be forgotten. Around five he came to his booth where Bruno and I waited for the call from headquarters.

"I'm hungry," he said. "Those bastards should forget about regulations and send us some food. I didn't even have breakfast."

This didn't actually amount to a capitulation to our cause, but it helped to dispel ignoble suspicions about his intentions.

At six o'clock, when hunger was already wreaking havoc on everyone, the colonel's voice abruptly came forth on the radio. For humanitarian considerations his superiors had authorized the delivery of food, sandwiches and some beverages. For this operation they would have to cut the electricity supply to the train's tracks.

We demanded that no more than two unarmed men, and if possible a member of the International Red Cross, come through the tunnel linked to the Salvador station, a strange suggestion put forth by Samuel. The colonel agreed. Except that for the hostages' benefit he would add a representative of national security. The news about an imminent supply of food was greeted with loud expressions of joy by all present, which could be interpreted as a definition of our guts' condition by that time.

Once the lights were cut off, Bruno and I took our places on the Salvador side to wait for the messengers. A few minutes later we saw the shining of their flashlight in the distance, at the end of the tunnel. We ordered them to raise their arms and walk slowly toward us.

"Don't shoot! We are unarmed!"

The request probably emanated from the alleged member of the Red Cross.

They came toward us with a military knapsack full of food

and canned beverages. The man from security—his hair in a military cut, his gaze oblique and evasive—knew how to perform his job.

"I demand to see the hostages. If not, I have orders to suspend negotiations."

"Just come in," Bruno replied defiantly. "Later on you can tell your bosses that we are civilized people, don't you agree?"

The Red Cross representative and I remained in the darkness. His name was Sanhueza, he said. He was young and seemed well-intentioned, proudly displaying his identifying health badges.

"It's a riot outside," he said, smiling with an air of complicity. "Everybody is glued to the radio and there are news flashes on the half hour. I'm sure I'll be in the newspapers tomorrow. My old lady will be proud."

"Your mother?"

"My wife."

"You're married?"

"Happily so," he confirmed. "And we have two kids."

"Good, and what do they say?"

"The kids?"

"The radio reports."

"Ah! Yes… First they said it was a students' prank. Later that the case was serious and that...you want to go to Cuba, eh?"

"That's correct."

The expression on his face veered from initial bafflement to the most fraternal commiseration. Then he made a beautiful turnabout.

"Well, to each his own, I say."

"That's the whole idea," I agreed.

"At six o'clock the Undersecretary of the Interior spoke on television. I feel duty-bound to inform you."

"What did he say?"

"You won't be offended?"

"Not at all."

"Well...he talked about an operation orchestrated by international Marxists."

"That's not very original."

"And that you are a bunch of lunatics," he said.

"That's more original."

"Now tell me…why in heaven's name did you hijack the metro? Wouldn't it have been better to grab a plane?"

I pondered for a moment, then had a flash of inspiration.

"Look. One can spend a whole life playing the Good Samaritan, Sanhueza, the way you do. Bandaging people, giving them painkillers, prescribing injections, delighted with that philanthropic routine. Later you confirm that wounded patients have recovered and the physician on the shift congratulates you, patting you on the back at the end of the month, do you follow me? Extremely conventional, including your salary. But one day you go home and discover…who knows? A naked man in the bedroom closet…And it turns out that the man is that same doctor."

"God forbid!"

"I agree, but it could happen, eh? And then what? Continue with the bandages, the shots and the usual painkillers? At that moment you might want to do something different, time to break out of the routine and choose an option. Never see the old lady again, never work again, no more birds in hand for security but hundreds flying around, with you having to pick one. Then…why not go far away? Why not board the Santiago metro and force the conductor to take you to another country? And why not Cuba over any other place?"

At that moment we heard the voices of Bruno and the security guy returning.

"I really don't understand you," Sanhueza concluded reasonably. "Anyhow I wish you a happy trip, to you and your colleagues."

"You are very kind."

"But those outside are thinking of attacking you, I must warn you."

"You said it before: to each his own."

"Of course. Well, it was a pleasure."

He began to move forwards to shake hands with me but he restrained himself when he sensed the man from security behind him, very close to us.

"Everything is in order," said the newcomer. "Let's go, Sanhueza."

"Tell your bosses," Bruno warned him, "that if they try an armed rescue, we'll kill the hostages, is that clear?"

"Crystal clear...if you have the guts for it."

They walked away through the tunnel and we remained still for a while in the dark, mesmerized by the swinging flashlights in the distance.

Then I said, "It's not true."

"About killing the hostages? No."

"So if they decide to attack...we're dead."

"Who knows," he sighed. "We wouldn't be losing much, don't you think? A well-calculated system of restrictions and punishments has gradually robbed us of life. That's exactly what's happened to us. Otherwise how can you understand all this, this rather disastrous ending? A hijacking with machine guns that could easily become a..."

He didn't finish the sentence. A skin crawling sensation hit my back, almost bowling me over in the darkness. If I had turned right then, I might have suddenly seen death, the shadow of death in back of me, waiting, indifferently watching me over my shoulder.

"Anyhow," he continued, "something makes a difference this way, I don't know quite why. There is a touch of redemption in all this, don't you think? Perhaps an overdue debt from the past, a collective gesture somehow gives us back the lost years, by the simple fact of locking ourselves up in an underground train, waiting for them to blow us up. We are, if you will, at the beginning of everything. For sure they will once more deny us the fact of being born. We'll be expelled from paradise, cut into little pieces if necessary... but they will not be able to return us ever again to the limbo of a useless life of submission. That guy walking down the tunnel to submit his report, he and his supervisors... they'd give anything to reverse the process, to return the metro to its normal course and wipe the smile off the passengers' faces, or demand that they swear allegiance to their faction and leave the coach once and for all. Then they'd erase our presence off the radios and television. They are totally incapable of understanding that somebody will die for the urge to hold them by their balls for a few hours. This is a duel, man, power to power, on equal terms, but something tells me that they lost it before it started."

He went back to the car. Something relaxed inside me. I dared turn my head and there wasn't even a shadow behind me, just the darkened train where Horacio was resuming his evening show and the hot red ember of a cigarette winked in the darkness. I remained alone in the tunnel a long while, immobile, going over all that had happened. I felt at peace, paradoxically serene. Then I returned to the train to share the last supper among friends.

They never turned on the lights in the tunnel. We distributed the food in the dark, using a flashlight provided by the conductor. We didn't have much appetite but Samuel insisted on the need to maintain our strength and consume the goods donated by the Department of the Interior. Around eleven o'clock Bruno started to lose patience and decided to use the radio to demand that the lights be switched on. The conductor pointed out that, generally, the radio didn't work without electricity.

Bruno emerged from the conductor's booth in a rage and ordered us to join him outside to discuss the situation. He was now issuing forceful commands. We had reached the typical military phase: the differences with our adversaries were fading, the shadows made all of us equal, the sons of darkness, lacking subtle discriminating traits.

Horacio and the Englishman remained in the car with the passengers, some of whom had already laid down to sleep on the seats.

"We are in the dark," said Bruno when we were outside.

"... and we are isolated," added Hugo.

"We are disgusting," declared Samuel with his natural tendency to self-criticism. "As guerrillas we are disgusting."

"The rather radiant expression on the hostages' faces," I said, "must have convinced the authorities that our threats are mostly a rhetorical exercise. They have decided to take the risk and leave us in the dark."

"What do we do now?" asked Hugo.

"We wait," suggested Bruno. "Sooner or later they will have to show signs of life..."

"Or death," remarked Samuel.

There was nothing much else to add and Bruno gave his orders for the evening.

"Two of us will guard each end of the coach until four o'clock. The rest may go inside and get some sleep. Tomorrow things are going to be tough and we must be wide awake."

The silence that followed proved that we agreed.

"I'll stay outside for the first shift," said Bruno. "I'll watch the Salvador side of the tunnel."

"I'll take the other side," added Hugo.

"Everybody rest now. We'll wake you up at four o'clock to take the next shift. This has been a memorable day, comrades," concluded our leader sadly. "May our health be with us until dawn."

"Quite improbable," commented Samuel.

We didn't speak anymore. Around two o'clock in the morning a commando of special forces entered the tunnel in two separate factions, one by the Salvador flank, the other from the Baquedano side. Coordinating their progress on a precise schedule, they crawled in the dark, in complete silence, until they were about twenty meters from the train on both sides, without our sentries ever detecting their presence. At a preestablished time they opened fire. Bruno was the first to fall. Hugo managed to return fire a couple of times but they got him in the legs. The din jerked us abruptly out of sleep. I saw the Englishman throwing himself out of the car, rushing toward the place where Hugo shouted something unintelligible. Panic spread among the passengers, a woman knelt down in the middle of the coach to pray aloud, a man stood up from the corner where he had been sleeping and came to me screaming for us not to kill them. Then I heard Horacio's voice screeching at the other end of the car: "It's judgment day, brother! Alleluia!"

I was paralyzed, unable to decide what to do, with Horacio yelling at the end of the car and the terrified clamor of the passengers all around me. I couldn't see Samuel, but somebody was answering the fusillade from the conductor's booth and it had to be him. As I recovered some aplomb, I issued orders to the hostages (get down on the floor, everybody down!) and I reached for my revolver inside my jacket while advancing toward the door. With spontaneous determination I jumped outside, my back against the car. From the Baquedano side, Hugo's voice reached me, yelling that he was wounded. Turning in the opposite direction I found the Englishman, his limp body leaning against the train's wheels. At that juncture I sensed a feline movement behind me and a blow with a rifle butt forced me to the ground.

"Just move, son of a bitch, and we'll squash you!"

I looked back and saw two silhouettes aiming at my head. Almost simultaneously the firing stopped.

It was finished.

The rest of the operation was just as swift. Our surrender completed, a throng rushed toward the train, a full division of shadows, their faces camouflaged with paint, springing out of the silence and the night, organizing their action to the call of flat orders, random shoving and now unnecessary threats. The hostages' presence stopped a promotion-seeking soldier from giving Hugo the coup de grâce. The beatings started right there in the tunnel, where those of us who were still standing received our first lesson in state justice, only a preamble to what would take place later. The complete pharmacopoeia on counterinsurgency would be dealt out in generous doses during the endless time spent in isolation within the regime's subterranean caverns. When they finally restored the electricity and lined us up against the tunnel wall, from the corner of my eye I saw Bruno and the Englishman on one side of the tracks, soaked in a fine rendering of blood droplets, traces of the battle that a metro employee would wipe away the next day. In the bewilderment of the moment I was overcome by the impossible desire to stay there, close to them, marveling at the serenity radiating from their faces, in that horizontal position that exempted them from the fangs of interrogations.

The hostages were evacuated first. Gathered in a ragged column of haggard faces, they were urged to walk toward the exit to the sound of intermittent commands. One of the women and the schoolgirls kept turning their tearful eyes to where we were lined up. In a way, we were victorious. Then it was our turn. Hugo was carelessly thrown on a stretcher. With machine guns pointed at our backs, we were forced to walk through the tunnel toward Salvador station, where we arrived in a few minutes.

At the foot of the stairs we were handcuffed. We had to wait a moment before getting out on the street because the place was crawling with reporters and those in charge of the operation didn't want photos taken.

The station was shining clean at that early hour. There wasn't a speck of dust on the tiles, nor a drop of blood or offending graffiti on the walls.

Except in one place. A small circle traced with a sharp instrument on the entrance wall. And inside the circle a single indelible sentence, clandestinely written by an anonymous hand that, in passing, had declared its allegiance to the dissidents' cause: "Power to the imagination. May 1980."

In a way, it was a victory.

Monday evening he started to write the last chapter of his *Brief History of Inca Civilization*. But the intimate satisfaction of the imminent conclusion of a task was blended this time with the intangible taste of desperation, besides his fatigue, a melancholic shadow that the recently discovered cardiac deficiency now placed on his life and residual toils at the Municipal Library of La Paz.

Things were not much better in the Inca Empire. Huáscar's rebellion had been quelled and his stepbrother, Atahualpa, governed a land always steeped in endless conflicts, denunciations, frightful rumors never confirmed of new confrontations with Huáscar's supporters. Meanwhile in Yucatán (how could they know in Cusco?), an advance guard of improvised deities had emerged from the sea some time earlier to invite the people to adopt their faith, a peculiar theology of crosses and dying martyrs. And at the exact time when their leader took possession of Tenochtitlán, another expedition departed southbound under the command of Pizarro and Almagro, both hungry for the honor denied them in Mexico.

It was hard to summarize all that—the imminent fall of the empire—in just a few pages that his students might later consult with no purpose other than to attain a passing grade in the subject, which he still taught in Salamanca, where he would finally return after this long, drawn-out two-year stay in La Paz. Without leaving the library and thanks to the local chroniclers, he had exhaustively explored the Andean massif from Ecuador to Atacama, stopping for some months in Quito before descending to Cusco and Machu Picchu, subsidized by a hardly worthless grant from the Spanish authorities that, five centuries later, covered his most elementary expenses and those of his wife in a well-to-do suburb of La Paz.

From the north the news had spread, as was to be expected, that white-skinned foreigners encased in strange caparisons were marching toward Cusco, riding uncommon quadrupeds, speaking in tongues foreign to the empire and other regions as well, intent on proclaiming the arrival of a new era, the fall and genesis, in Cusco and Tungasuca, in Carabaya and the Watanay river, in the four regions of the empire, the culmination of the ancestral wait for progress and the Bible.

Thirty long years of explorations similar to this one, of meticulous investigation into the written testimonies of all epochs (a reiterated chronicle of domination), didn't fully convince him or reveal the ultimate goal that might allow him to perceive, once and for all, what his university colleagues pompously referred to as "the motor of history." Could it be the civilizing obsession mingled with its protagonists' less laudable ambitions? Or perhaps vengeance, the desire of the rebellious poor to recoup their losses, a feeling that momentarily made them strong and later instilled new urges for revenge in the next generation of downtrodden? Every deliberate synthesis now seemed a well-conceived but sterile fallacy, only useful in obtaining reasonable grants from the civic authorities.

A bit after six, earlier than usual, he left his office and walked to the front desk.

The librarian expressed surprise.

"You are already leaving, Professor? So early?"

"Yes, I'm leaving. I need to clear my mind a bit."

For a few seconds he scrutinized the copper-hued face with its almond shaped eyes. "The ancestry," he thought, "to whom I'm just an old fellow born on the opposite side of the Atlantic, who requests books covered with cobwebs in which his ancestors swarm with scant prestige."

He would soon leave that face to return—blessed be the day—to his classes in Salamanca.

"I'll leave with you, Professor," said Mamani. "It's already time."

Although they didn't converse, the discreet company of the employee helped calm him down on their way to the parking lot. On the ground floor they wished each other a good evening and

Aragon proceeded to his car. The warm evening air was his best ally at that time of the day, with the altiplano's stimulating atmosphere, and the eternally snowcapped Illimani in the distance.

Once he reached the parking lot something called his attention toward the building's fifth floor where his office was located.

"The light," he thought, peeved.

His office window—the narrow cubicle assigned to him by the local city hall about two years earlier—was lit, the only one on the fifth floor, something, by the way, quite unusual. He never forgot to turn it off.

He went down the Avenida del Prado toward Obrajes. On the sidewalks pedestrians and workers waited to be carried by the dozens to peripheral sectors of the city, or to the heights where water was scarce and the adobe houses piled up in the dust. From his side of the glass all of it seemed strangely new, even those well-known places he drove through daily, on the road from his home in Obrajes to the library and back. The civic employee seemed multiplied endlessly in the crowd of faces bunched together outside the car, the deep dark skin, the piercing eyes and thick hair, the hard, impassive expressions, apparently disdainful, watching him with somber haughtiness at every street corner.

"The ancestry," Aragon reiterated inwardly while something basically indefinable tugged at his guileless heart from street to street, from one face to another.

***

The next day, he thought he sensed a shade of disapproval in Mamani's morning greeting. As usual, the librarian had arrived a few minutes before him and probably discovered his failure to turn off the lights in the office. Anyhow, he opted to avoid any attempt at justification. The dignity inherent to his work in handling archives and his academic titles suggested the wisdom of keeping his distance from the staff. All things considered, Mamani himself was just an underling.

That morning he concentrated on Pizarro and the first internal disagreements in the expedition, described in detail by

Burke. This time Almagro was the loser and he departed for the south, searching for Chile. Burke himself made reference to the first attempt at an Indian rebellion, naturally unsuccessful, commanded south of Cusco by Huamán Quispe, the only leader who had managed to slip through the siege laid around the rebels by the conquistadors.

Close to noon he left his office for a light snack. While walking by the front desk he reconsidered his arrogant attitude that morning.

"Look, Mamani, about the light," he explained with some embarrassment, "it has never happened to me before. I never forget to turn it off and..."

Mamani looked at him, baffled.

"I don't understand, Professor."

"I'm speaking about the light in my office. Didn't you turn it off this morning when you came in?"

"No."

"No?"

"No."

"Ah! well...I would have sworn. But it's not important."

In the afternoon he continued reading Burke's feverish description. Manco II, hiding in Vilcabamba, Tupac Amaru and others prolonging the saga of failed uprisings all over the empire. The material concerning their heroic feats absorbed him well into the evening when everybody was already gone, including Mamani. At seven, perhaps later, he thought of his wife's probable anger, checked that everything was in order and left the office. The library was dark and empty. Having almost reached the door, something in the air drew his attention, between the aisles and the bookshelves. The old smell of the assembled volumes now hit his nose with unexpected intensity. It mingled with other odors until then undetected: incense perhaps, and sweat, all of it concentrated in the semidarkness of the fifth floor, probably the lingering scent of the last readers, a penetrating, insidious stench that permeated the whole library, treacherously assaulting his nostrils, following him to the exit and down the stairs, like a beast that had been lurking in a corner.

"The ancestry," he thought again, half amused and half worried, finally leaving the building and walking toward the parking lot. "Perhaps the ventilation system is not working."

When he approached the car his heart gave a start. The light in his office window was on, the only one shining in the whole building.

"Now what..." he said to himself impatiently.

Any probability of forgetting to turn it off was now discarded: someone (the smell!) had stealthily invaded his office. Someone who watched him at his work, who waited in hiding somewhere on the fifth floor and was right now enjoying his notes. Crushed, he walked toward the booth next to the parking lot looking for the night sentry to explain what was going on.

"It's impossible, Professor," the man concluded skeptically, without leaving his booth. "Nobody comes in at this time."

"Come with me and see for yourself, man," Aragon insisted.

They walked to his car to look from there at the building's facade. It was now pitch dark.

"You see?" observed the guard.

"It can't be. Only a minute ago it was..."

Aragon demanded angrily that he use his keys to go with him to his office to verify that everything was in order. The man reluctantly agreed and they walked together toward the building. Having arrived at the fifth floor, Aragon noticed uneasily that the smell he had detected earlier still lingered among the bookshelves.

On the other hand his office was pitch dark and his papers were in order where he had left them before leaving. The guard remarked—interrupting himself to yawn—that his duty required that he return promptly to his booth. Aragon imagined him telling his companions the next day about the incident ("The old man has a screw loose from so much reading!") among mocking laughter and gross jeers meant to chafe his most basic sense of pride.

"You work too hard, Professor," the guard diagnosed.

Aragon felt annoyed.

"What are you suggesting? That window was lit, man, I'm not crazy, nor do I have visions. Somebody was here and I will hold you responsible if so much as one page of this manuscript is missing, is that clear?"

He arbitrarily piled up his papers, only to leave them as they were.

"Come on, let's get out of here. The air is intolerable."

He didn't even comment on the incident to his wife. That night he dreamed of the altiplano, in it a rocky trail and on one side an individual who had collapsed by the road. At his side was an old man writing down a report on this fact, taking endless notes and then explaining something related to history and acts of retaliation. Upon awakening, he only remembered the face of the fallen man, the same features that he had seen the night before, infinitely multiplied on the sidewalks of La Paz.

He pondered that one Indian was, all things considered, very much like another, all Indians the same Indian...All things considered.

***

"Good morning, Professor. Did you sleep well?"

The obvious irony in Mamani's tone of voice confirmed what Aragon perceived when leaving the parking lot and climbing the stairs. The mocking glances between the employees, their elemental complicity about elemental matters, perhaps the sentry's description to his work companions first thing in the morning, telling in his own way what had happened yesterday evening.

Without thinking further about what didn't deserve undue attention, he closed the door to his office behind him. Burke dwelt upon the preceding day's rebellion and the return of Huamán Quispe to the plantations. It was a matter of record that he had later gotten lost in the jungle on the Bolivian side, followed by horrendous legends about his capture, invariably refuted by several aboriginal uprisings north of Tiawanaku, with Huamán Quispe slipping time and again through the siege, much to the bafflement of the chroniclers that Burke himself quoted, none of whom could confirm his capture with absolute certainty.

Anxious to put an end to his work, Aragon decided to postpone eating until evening and didn't go downstairs for lunch. In the afternoon, he started to write down his conclusions—the balance, that is—with the characteristic deliberation of his style, reporting now about a "civilizing advance never before equaled in history, with the unexpected marriage of Christ and Pachamama, the local pagan deity that, in its consubstantial spontaneity has managed to resist to this day the multitudinarian process of catechization carried out by the European missionaries in the American subcontinent."

At the last minute, he cast aside the detailing of the failed Indian rebellion, Burke's adherence to the anecdotal and superfluous, the futile vicissitudes of certain local chieftains, except in what concerned Huamán Quispe, whom he described in half a page of temperate commendations. In the library, empty once more by evening, Aragon stopped the irrepressible oscillation of his pen and re-read his last sentence. He had finished.

Satisfied, although not exultant, he placed his papers inside his briefcase and then stood up with it under his arm. He turned off the desk lamp and felt his way among the bookshelves toward the exit, unperturbed.

Then he smelled the odor, that sweet and wild aroma, the mixture of underarm sweat and other essences that had caught his attention the night before and now seemed to spread with greater intensity among the bookshelves, once more overshadowing his personal accomplishment, turning it—exactly—into a last paroxysm of irritation. Or rather fear, the same feeling experienced on preceding days, once more fear, his heart bucking wildly in his old and frail chest when suddenly he realized he was lost in the penumbra of the fifth floor, sure that somebody lurked nearby among the bookshelves, while he couldn't find the way out, overcome by the nauseating stench emanating from the back of the room, just there, where he seemed to detect something, a silhouette, the sketchy, wavering form of some local figure, scarcely able to perceive the almond eyes, the implacable stare in the unyielding face that watched him.

"Who are you?" he screamed. "What are you looking for,

damn it!"

He didn't expect an answer and didn't get one. He tried to fling himself in search of the exit door, getting lost among the bookshelves, his heart bolting inside him, exerting increasing pressure on his chest. He felt like he was choking. He felt an excruciating pain inside him. He felt...

The news appeared in the social life section of *Presencia* and other dailies the day after the event. It included the succinct statement by José Mamani, the Municipal Library employee who found him the next day lying between the bookshelves, his heart exploded by an infarction, the manuscript near his body. The city authorities in La Paz gave assurances that it would be published as a posthumous homage to the author, including the passage about Huamán Quispe, whose capture was never confirmed in the chronicles of his era.

epilogue

Imitating Borges' well-known fondness for last minute remarks, I write the following lines overflowing with pride—perhaps too close to gratitude or even conceit. *Our Neighbor's Last Days* is a tactless joke at the expense of a good friend who survived a frightful diagnosis. *Pharaoh Exposed* turned out to be a convoluted history lesson which I enjoyed writing immensely. This also happened with *All the Horses In Toulon Go around Naked*, probably my most elaborate narration, whose main character relapses in the least publicized street activities of J.J. Rousseau. A highly respected panel of experts awarded it, in its day, an important prize, a decision that still pleases me and which, on that occasion, drove away the dark beast of poverty from our door in Madrid. Those are the times when literature wraps itself in mystique. Later we long again for those moments. *A Man Eight Years Older* deliberately twists the fascinating story of Carlos Iriart, who seemed to have sprung, in his innate kindness, from the pages of Osvaldo Soriano. *The Last Supper* has its roots in Madrid after a most significant dialogue with Maria Jesus Lozano, to whom I feel deeply indebted for her friendship. I published it in a first version with some variations: the Dutch hero had another name and was at the time a rabid Calvinist, but a friend warned me in time that in the Protestant tradition the crosses don't display the figure of Christ and his wounds. Therefore I had to convert that wandering Dutchman to Catholicism thus adjusting to the demands of the story. *Anniversary* insists on an obsession for indigenous gastronomy and the "bearded gods from beyond the oceans." Without them, many of us would still be running around in loincloths although we would have rid ourselves of their angry God. At this point, neither concept matters: Spain is my second motherland, a fact somehow refuted by the ghostly character of the *Ancestry*. *Entropy* redeems me from the long hours spent on innumerable translations, relying on a very real group of "clochards" almost devoid of words because freedom always seems to me, brief, too brief. The idea which triggered *A Businessman Disappears* was given to me by Julio Ollero who—without a good reason—distrusted his capacity as a narrator. This proved invaluable to those who took refuge under his skillful editor's mantle. *Gray Danube* and *An Empty Cage* both take place in Viena among whose parks and narrow streets paved with stones I spent a summer. The first story presents a whimsical profile of Freud that the Iberian version of *Playboy* deemed worthy of a prize. The second is an homage to a certain orangutan restricted to the Schonbrunn Zoo whose unalterable dignity behind bars made me think of a particular Kafkesque personality bent on starving. There must be a connection between the orangutan and Freud which escapes me right now. In the final analysis, one writes from a kind of penumbra— especially when the narration refers to our most private parts, which happens in both stories. *King of the Jungle* reflects, in its own way, on the final collapse of the Soviet Union; now, sadly enough, the only question which still remains is what to do with the complete works of Lenin. *The Lost Years* is a story of times past, a slave of its own doctrine, that insists—perhaps at the wrong moment—on the psychological effects of institutional terror and the pathetic state of its subjects. I published it some time ago in a more naïve version, certainly more helpless than the present one. It might be that its only merit was the naïveté of old times. *Round Trip* is a blatant tribute to Carlos Fuentes and his pristine narrator's spirit. *Visitor's Day* delves into similar longings found in every corner of nostalgic memories when one is confronted with an empty pillow. It is—once more—people on the prowl, if only of memories.